No Rot

20

ON A STILL NIGHT

In California, British avionics expert
Christopher Ward is leading an
enquiry into the tragic disappearance
of passenger aircraft working Pacific
routes when he falls victim to an
unexplained attempt on his life. The
subsequent cancellation of Ward's
project forces him to begin his own
search far into the South Pacific,
where he witnesses the terrible reason
behind the loss of so many lives.
Amidst the lagoons and reefs, Ward is
faced with a desperate fight for his
own survival. Unless he can escape,
his secret will die with him.

COLIN D. PEEL

ON A STILL NIGHT

Complete and Unabridged

LINFORD
Leicester

First published in Great Britain in 1975 by
Robert Hale Limited
London

First Linford Edition
published 2003
by arrangement with
Robert Hale Limited
London

British Library CIP Data

Peel, Colin D. (Colin Dudley), *1936* –
On a still night.—Large print ed.—
Linford mystery library
1. Detective and mystery stories
2. Large type books
I. Title
823.9′14 [F]

ISBN 0–7089–9468–7

Published by
F. A. Thorpe (Publishing)
Anstey, Leicestershire

Set by Words & Graphics Ltd.
Anstey, Leicestershire
Printed and bound in Great Britain by
T. J. International Ltd., Padstow, Cornwall

This book is printed on acid-free paper

For Pen and Jo

1

There was nothing exceptional to mark the departure of Flight P.Y.432 from Los Angeles on this Sunday evening, apart from a forty minute delay in loading. At this time of year, so close to Christmas, severe congestion both inside and outside the passenger terminals is not uncommon and the delay had been building up in the intercontinental section since early morning. Previous flights from gate 27A had been forced to wait for connecting aircraft which in turn had been held up at their own points of departure. Flight P.Y.432 had been delayed by circumstances created simply by a season of the year and by nothing else — it was a matter of no significance whatever.

At exactly eleven twenty five hours on December the seventeenth, twenty first class passengers and one hundred and twenty economy class passengers neatly packaged and strapped securely to their seats waited for their Boeing 707 to begin its take-off.

One of the world's most reliable and best tested long range aircraft, the 707-338C started to taxi as soon as the captain received his clearance from flight control. Minutes later, one hundred and ten tons of sophisticated equipment left the ground carrying its precious cargo of humanity outwards over the Pacific.

The 338C carries nineteen thousand eight hundred and fifty gallons of aviation fuel which it consumes at the rate of one thousand six hundred and forty gallons per hour giving it a range of about five thousand miles. It has two independent polar path compass systems working in conjunction with a Doppler radar whilst a flight director supplies visual information on altitude, direction and flight requirements. In addition to this equipment there is the radio and the weather radar. This late model 707 is an extremely safe aircraft and cannot under any normal circumstances deviate from its predetermined flight path by accident.

Beneath the floor of the cabin, in the

belly of the plane, is the cargo hold —
over two thousand cubic feet of it — and,
although there was little space to spare on
P.Y.432, the compartment was certainly
no more densely packed than usual.

Fully loaded, the plane climbed slowly
through the Californian night to an
altitude of thirty nine thousand feet
leaving the lights of L.A. and the west
coast of the United States far behind as it
began the long haul to Papeete.

Hostess Susan Baker was tired and
irritable. The party last night had lasted
well into the early hours of the morning
and she was angry for allowing herself to
have been pursuaded to go to bed with
the good looking U.C.L.A. student called
Roy. As it turned out, he had been
something of a disappointment which she
was quite sure was causing much of the
inward annoyance that she was experiencing at the moment.

She smiled automatically at the coarse
featured Australian in 33F, feeling his
eyes slide inside the open neck of her
blouse as she leaned forward with the
bourbon.

'I'll bring your change later, sir.'

36C next, gin and tonic and a coke for the schoolgirl with the glasses in the window seat. Then the whiskies for the three well dressed Frenchmen, knowing that she would have to lean over again. There were times, she thought bitterly, when she was tempted to board a flight without her bra — just so the passengers would get their moneys worth.

Someone was tapping her shoulder.

'Sue, do you have any rum? — I need three.' It was Wendy Holmes, the hostess from the first class section. She had been at the party too but had left early with the 747 pilot whom she had been dating regularly for the past three or four months.

Sue Baker's answer was drowned by the loudest wail that the baby in 34B had yet produced.

'Help yourself, Wendy — it's on the trolley,' she said shortly before squeezing past to find out from the parents if anything was needed.

Seated in the rear of the plane, the group of fresh faced boys — a swimming team from Nevada on their way to New Zealand — started singing noisily again. Within three quarters of an hour from take-off, they had drunk enough to become a nuisance and it required the attention of all three economy class hostesses to quieten them.

Immediately in front of the boys sat an elderly English couple on their way to visit their daughter in Sydney and beside them, some rather pretty Tahitian girls, returning home after failing to make a fortune from two years solid prostitution in San Francisco, talked quietly amongst themselves.

Businessmen rubbed shoulders with schoolchildren, grandmothers ate the plastic airline dinner whilst chatting to young men with occupations in the Pacific islands that would have made their hair turn even whiter if they had known and parents struggled to suppress the incessant crying of their babies. The passengers of P.Y.432 were typical enough and in no way exceptional. There were no celebrities on board and there was not a single gentleman in first class that appeared in any way distinguished.

Once the dinner trays had been collected and the queues for the toilets had reduced to not more than five or six anxious people, the captain was advised that the time was appropriate for him to make his customary address. After experimenting for several weeks with a voice modelled on John Wayne, tonight Captain James Murray felt sufficiently confident to try it out in public for the first time. He flipped the switch to interrupt the circuits carrying piped music to those passengers who had been pursuaded to rent earphones, cleared his throat impressively and began with a slow drawl.

'Ladies and gentlemen,' he growled, realising that if anything he had pitched it a little too low, 'this is Captain Murray speaking. We shall be dimming the lights shortly and rather than interrupting your sleep I thought it better to give you a brief run down on our flight right now. I must apologise for the delay in our departure which was caused by circumstances beyond our control — however, we should make up some of the time on the first leg of our flight to Tahiti. Our estimated arrival time in Papeete is four thirty eight hours and our stop over there will be about two hours before proceeding onwards to Auckland and Sydney. I have no weather report on Tahiti at present but as many of you will know there is little variation in conditions there at this time of year. For those of you who are interested, I'll be sending back a copy of our flight plan shortly from which you will see that our route takes us just about straight from L.A. to Papeete across the Pacific passing well north of the Marquesas islands.

'That's about all I have to say right now so I'll wish you a pleasant flight and bid you good night.'

Wendy Holmes poked her head through the door to the flight deck.

'Marvellous — absolutely marvellous,' she said with genuine admiration, 'I don't know how you do it.'

James Murray grinned at her. 'Maybe I should've taken up drama after all — at least I'd sleep nights instead of doing this,' he nodded at the glowing instruments.

'Not with all those dolly actresses around.' Wendy Holmes pulled the door shut and went back to tuck up her expensive first class passengers.

Soon it was silent inside the big jet, most of the passengers sprawling awkwardly in their reclined seats, attempting to relieve the boredom by forcing themselves to sleep.

Here and there a reading light burned in the darkened cabin and occasionally one of the babies in the hammocks that hung from the luggage rack would awake to cry for a few minutes only to be rocked quickly back to sleep.

In the tail, now totally exhausted after serving forty dinners, Susan Baker recounted a suitably edited version of her experiences from the previous night to two disinterested members of flight service.

Leaving a vapour trail in the darkness nearly ten miles long, P.Y.432 pushed on unseen through the night on its unexceptional routine flight across the ocean at a speed slightly in excess of five hundred and seventy miles per hour.

★   ★   ★

At two thirty on the morning of December the eighteenth, two and a half hours away from Tahiti, the cabin lights slowly brightened whilst the hostesses moved efficiently up and down the fuselage waking those passengers who had been fortunate enough to snatch a few hours fitful sleep.

Blankets and pillows were returned to the luggage racks, bottles were warmed for the babies and aspirins were dispensed to the gentlemen who had not managed to sleep off the effects of excessive alcohol.

In one of the seats reserved for non-smokers at the front of the economy class cabin, an elderly American lady from Kansas was insisting that the stout gentleman across the aisle had been secretly puffing on cigarettes during the time that the lights had been out. Wendy Holmes, who had a sick passenger requiring attention in the first class section, had been called back to deal with the problem in order to allow the economy flight service girls to serve the chilled orange juice that preceded breakfast.

Stretching for nearly one third of the way down the rear of the aircraft, the queue for the toilets lengthened to a stable maximum making it totally impossible for Sue Baker to leave the galley with the breakfast trays.

On the flight deck, Captain Murray thought of the three rest days ahead of him in Tahiti, wondering whether the girl from Moorea would telephone him at the hotel as she had promised. Knowing that on a flight as full as this chaos would exist for at least the next hour amongst the passengers until the morning meal was over, he refrained from making his standard good morning speech, attending instead to the boring routine that his job demanded he follow. His crew had stopped talking to each other some time ago having exhausted most of the topics of conversation which were in any way mutually interesting and a general air of fatigue filled the small cabin.

At precisely two fifty one, Tahitian time, shortly before James Murray was due to make his first scheduled radio call to flight control in Papeete, the entirely unexceptional nature of Flight 432 suddenly and dramatically changed.

The immediate effect of the change was not detected by the one hundred and forty tired and dehydrated passengers for several minutes, although, if the blinds had been open on the port side, it might just have been possible for an intelligent observer to have become curious at the two sudden streaks of light that flared briefly in the night sky.

Senior hostesses for the two cabins were summoned urgently to the flight deck where they were briefed. Three and a half minutes later, Captain Murray turned on the microphone to address his passengers. This time, unnoticed, he spoke with the soft Washington voice learnt from his childhood.

'Ladies and gentlemen, I have to make you aware of a very serious situation that has developed on this flight.

'Owing to a gross malfunction of our fuel supply system and our failure to rectify the fault over the last hour, it is going to be necessary for me to take the plane down onto the water at once.'

His voice became stern, although a slight tremor was detectable at the end of certain words.

'I must ask you to remain calm and from this moment onwards on no account to leave your seats for any reason at all. Those of you who are waiting for the toilet should return to your seats inside the next five minutes whether or not nature has been satisfied.

'I shall be contacting flight control at Faaa in the next few minutes and I can tell you that when we make our final approach run, the aircraft will be within a quarter of a mile of a surface vessel that I am already in touch with by radio.

'Please put on your life jackets now in the way that you have been shown and I must insist that you again carefully study the leaflet in the seat pocket in front of you, which describes the correct procedure to follow for a forced landing at sea. Your hostesses will remind you of the means of egress from the aircraft and the crew will be responsible for opening the exits when I issue the command to do so.

'As you know, sufficient life rafts to accept all of the passengers and crew of this aircraft are contained behind panels in the ceiling above you — these will be launched by the crew and will inflate automatically on contact with the water.

'In order for this operation to be successful, it is essential for all of you to remain as calm as you possibly can and to do exactly what the flight crew request. There is no cause for panic — a landing on calm sea, whilst by no means a routine occurrence, can be carried out with minimal risk.

'I shall be talking to you again before making the final descent.'

The passengers of P.Y.432 reacted to the news that their lives had suddenly become extremely insecure in a predictable manner.

Hopelessly, the flight service girls

watched the reaction begin, knowing that unless they were able to control the spreading panic there would be no chance of saving either the lives of passengers or their own.

With a dreadful weak feeling centred in her stomach, Susan Baker tried to remember her training. Three types — the normally frightened, those whose panic would gradually build to an uncontrollable pitch and the artificially super brave. All three would be here somewhere and only the first type was safe.

Standing alone at the front of her section of the economy cabin, ready to demonstrate the correct way of fitting and inflating the life jacket for the second time on this flight, she was acutely conscious of the fact that for the very first time in her career these instructions were to be of critical importance and no mere formality. A sea of frightened faces stared expectantly at her from the seats, waiting for the words she would speak into the microphone that she grasped unsteadily in her moist hand.

The gasps, the initial shock reactions

were over now and the full horror of the situation was beginning to be felt. Quickly she started the demonstration, deftly slipping the life jacket over her head whilst automatically delivering the instructions she knew so well.

Some of the jackets failed to withdraw easily from their compartments beneath the seats. Despite perfectly clear instructions, nearly a third of the passengers appeared to be unable to tie the laces correctly and three people had stupidly pulled the inflation tabs already making it almost impossible for them to move in their seats.

'Please return to your seat sir — ' she stared pointedly at a middle aged man who had walked from the rear of the cabin.

A confident smile flickered across his face. 'I think I'll be able to help you,' he said seriously, 'I am not frightened.'

Here's one, thought Susan Baker, a super brave for sure.

'Look,' she said firmly, 'anyone who's not frightened is stupid — now get back to your seat, I haven't time to argue.' She turned, hoping that the sick fear had not shown in her eyes.

A young woman was crying softly somewhere and behind her a male voice was repeating the words 'Oh God,' over and over again. Unable to cope with the fear generated by a hundred and forty terrified people, the overloaded air conditioning system was allowing a faint stench of perspiration to leak back into the feed ducting and it seemed as though the cabin temperature was increasing as the plane lost altitude.

Sensing the aura of fear, all of the babies were crying now, adding to the confusion that the hostesses were striving to reduce.

A flabby man with thick lips, seated near one of the centre exits, held both hands over the red weals on his face caused by a successfully vicious slash from the handful of stereo earphones that one of the hostesses was collecting. Feeling a hand slide between her thighs as she stopped to tighten the seat belt of a small boy, she had turned and swiped at the same time. Vaguely she recalled something about this type of sexual reaction to prolonged fear from a lecture long ago in training school.

The captain's voice crackled briefly over the speakers. 'Okay flight service — a final check of crash positions and return to your own locations, we're going down now — good luck everyone.'

Many of the women were sobbing uncontrollably by this time and there was a good deal of frightened swearing from certain seats. A few people had vomited, causing an unpleasant odour to further contaminate the already stuffy air.

With seat belts tightened until they hurt, with heads pushed hard onto the cushions supported on their knees and with arms wrapped around their heads, they waited as the 707 increased its dive angle.

The speed of descent was very much swifter than normal. Her fuel jettisoned long ago and with her flaps down, the nose of the aircraft now tipped down-wards even further. Violent pressure differences caused acute pain for many people but there was no change in the foetal attitudes of the passengers.

'Ten seconds — ' a terse message.

Married men thought of their wives and children safe in their homes thousands of miles away. Women carrying babies inside them tried to cushion their stomachs more effectively. Strong men cursed the airline, their anger at the possibility of death apparently greater than their fear.

Some thought of the futility of life, others suddenly and perhaps wonderfully realised how very precious it had become. But it was fear, unadulterated, undiluted naked fear that swept through the cabins, touching every crouching shoeless figure as they waited.

Feet above the sea, Murray actuated the hydraulic rams that would swing the reverse thrust baffles over the jet exhausts. P.Y.432 shuddered as the streams of hot gas blasted forwards to fight the massive inertia of the plane. Attempting a stall in level flight, in order to prevent the Pacific either from peeling off the skin of the fuselage or crushing the airframe like a toothpaste tube, Murray opened his throttles to maximum thrust.

The shrieking gas turbines accelerated to maximum boost, hurling enormous quantities of hot gas at the reverse thrust scoops, making the wings twist against the stiffness of the fuselage.

And then, as the first crest of the first cool wave licked the belly of P.Y.432, Murray dropped it.

One hundred and ten tons of steel and aluminium ploughed into the sea, creating a tremendous cloud of spray that reached up and back over the tail of the aircraft.

Gallons of cold water spewed into the engine intakes where it contacted stainless steel alloys running at red heat and rotating at extremely high speed. The result was explosive, the nightmare of screaming steel being abruptly snuffed out as the four engines nacelles were torn from the wing structure by the drag of the water.

Viewed from a distance, the landing would have appeared spectacular — even graceful — but inside the aircraft, the series of low frequency jolts to the fuselage of terrifying magnitude told another story.

The incredible noise of the tortured plane pushing tons of sea water in front of it as it attempted to flatten the gentle swell of the Pacific at an initial speed of just under one hundred miles per hour, drowned the cries of the passengers.

And then strangely it was still, even the babies reducing their howls to a muted whisper. P.Y.432 was down, floating in an unnatural environment, but floating nevertheless. Her precious human cargo was intact — not unhurt — but by and large not severely harmed.

The cabin lights had fused long ago and it was very dark inside.

After what seemed like a delay of several minutes, the flight crew pulled themselves together enough to stagger to the escape exits, finding their way by the flickering illumination from emergency flashlights. A nauseating smell of urine and excreta filled the cabins and the anguished groans of the injured interrupted the shouted pleas of the hostesses for all passengers to remain calm and seated until the hatches were pushed open.

Miraculously, few people had suffered serious injury. A vessel of some kind was apparently standing by to offer assistance. The aircraft would float well enough, trapped air preventing sea water from flooding into the rents in the skin for at least a while — the worst was over.

This time it was relief that coursed through the plane — even disbelief that everything had turned out all right. To have survived was a sweet almost elating experience for most people.

Locking arms fitted to hatches over the wings were unfastened first, to be followed by one on the starboard side near the tail. None of the others would work, the airframe having twisted suffi-ciently to jam the big levers solidly in their sockets.

Dizzy from the battering she had received whilst strapped in her seat, Sue Baker, thankful to be alive, stood at the door she was about to open, anticipating the smell of the moist sea air. It was the last breath she would ever take.

Although it was difficult to see clearly in the dark, several passengers observed the pretty hostess sink to her knees prior to collapsing onto the sill of the hatchway. Before any action could be taken, death had started to creep into the fuselage, visiting each row of seats in turn.

Seven minutes later, all life on board had been completely extinguished.

By dawn, no trace of P.Y.432 remained on the calm blue surface of the South Pacific.

2

Christopher Ward was angry. Half an hour of solid explanation had apparently been wasted, the other members of the meeting refusing to seriously consider the approach that he and Joanne had suggested. He waited for Dr. Joseph Bateman to finish speaking before pushing back his chair to stand up. The gesture had the desired effect, everyone staring at him wondering what had prompted such behaviour.

Although fairly tall — Ward stood just half an inch under six feet without his shoes on — he tended to give the impression of being somewhat fragile and the small pointed beard added little maturity to his youthful features. With the exception of Joanne Varick, who faced him across the wide expanse of glass topped table a faint smile hovering characteristically at the corners of her mouth, Ward knew that at thirty two he must easily be the youngest representative at the meeting. In order to make his point, a careful choice of words would be essential.

'Gentlemen,' he said quietly, no trace of the anger that he felt being transmitted to his voice, 'I have sat here since ten o'clock this morning and I have listened carefully to all of the proposals that have been put forward and with great patience I have waited until each has been dissected to death. If no one is prepared to be constructive and make a decision — any decision — then it seems that Miss Varick and I have travelled half way round the world for nothing.

'Before leaving London, both of us were led to believe that we had been invited to attend this meeting by special request. If, having spoken to us, you are of the opinion that our limited skills cannot be used to further your enquiries, then — with the greatest respect — for Christ's sake say so.'

An awkward silence filled the room, the muted hum from the air-conditioning seeming to increase in volume.

24

At the head of the table, representing the interests of three international carriers from the United States, the chairman of the meeting thought that the young Englishman had summed up the situation rather well. Frank Macklin was not offended at what amounted to a criticism of his chairmanship, instead, although realising that he should not have allowed matters to deteriorate to this point, he welcomed the outburst — hoping that from now on some more plain speaking could be expected.

He smiled at Ward, knowing how difficult it must have been for the young man to stand up in front of twenty three experts and give them all a blast.

'You're right, Chris,' he said, 'decisions are what we need, but maybe all of our comments need an airing first — I'd hate us to go off half cocked and we've all come a long way to Australia — let's make real sure that we know what we're doing before we start doing it. Now sit down and calm down and we'll see where we are.'

Despite a difference of twenty degrees

Fahrenheit between the temperature inside the conference room of the South Pacific headquarters of International Airline Security and the outside air in Sydney at this time of year, it was still unbearably hot. Delegates to the meeting from the northern hemisphere were to an extent enjoying the change, but the two representatives from Qantas and the gentleman from Air New Zealand seemed annoyed at what they considered to be intolerable working conditions.

Four European, three American and two Australasian airlines had sent representatives to this important meeting. With them, around the long table, sat an assortment of specialists in the field of flight security, some of them from Military Intelligence, others experts in accident analysis, whilst four gentlemen who had been responsible for a prolonged study of aircraft hijacking methods had also been invited to participate.

Joanne Varick, the single woman at the meeting, had accompanied Christopher Ward from London two weeks ago in order to carry out a preliminary survey of

Australian records covering all recent southern hemisphere aircraft accidents before attending this gathering of interested parties in Sydney. She was an acknowledged expert in the field of correlation theory, a branch of statistics or statistical methods as it is sometimes called. Specialising in multiple correlation where many variables may contribute to the cause of an event, she had spent five years researching into spurious correlation, teetering on the edge of conventional statistical theory.

Besides a fine mathematical brain and a good degree from Cambridge, Christopher Ward possessed an unusual and unwritten qualification that had, in a very short time, taken him close to the top of the technical stream in the European headquarters of the I.A.S. — the organisation responsible for the security of the hundreds of intercontinental flights made every week from European terminals. Ward's qualification was exceptional in an ever increasing environment of specialist thinkers. Ward was a doer — a rare product of the academic training that modern universities provide. Using extremely sophisticated technical, scientific and mathematical techniques, Ward had gained an enviable reputation as a problem solver for the past seven years. By using his brain and his unbounding energy in the challenging field of civil aviation in the autumn of the twentieth century, he had made significant contributions to methods used for air traffic control, automatic landing, flight direction and simulator design. More recently, Ward had been active in the analysis of procedures for hijacking prevention and it had become obvious that the young man was destined for great things but for one rather large shortcoming. Christopher Ward was too interested in too many subjects, his inquisitive mind continually diverting his attention to matters unconnected with his job.

Today, Ward felt warmly confident of his ability to produce answers to the serious problem that these men had gathered to discuss. It must be said that his close association with attractive

Joanne Varick on the project had rein-
forced his view that correlation theory
was the key to solving the equations
which would perhaps offer an explanation
for the mysterious and terrible air
disasters that had occurred over recent
months in the South Pacific basin.

An unconcealed wink from his pretty
colleague dispersed his anger and Ward
sat down again hoping that some of the
older men at the conference would stop
blustering and listen to the proposals that
Macklin was repeating.

Using the report which had been
prepared before the meeting, Macklin
again outlined the suggestion that the
English team of Ward and Varick should
be provided with a brief to undertake a
total investigation into every conceivable
event which had preceded the tragic loss
of each of the four passenger aircraft that
had vanished without trace since June of
last year. When every single piece of
information — whether or not it appeared
relevant — had been gathered and filed,
the English couple would carry out a
thorough analysis using Joanne's skill in

correlation theory. Computer techniques would be employed extensively in an attempt to generate a common pattern that would fit each accident.

A programme of this kind requires the services of a very large number of people mostly as information gatherers, but computer programmers, statisticians, clerks, aeronautical engineers and meteorological experts would also be needed. To co-ordinate a project of this magnitude, someone possessing the talents of Christopher Ward would be required and Ward, already anticipating the challenge of the job, was eager to begin.

Two thirds of the funds to cover the work would be provided by the airlines, the remaining cash being drawn from the substantial resources of International Air Security. The meeting had already agreed to the allocation of an unlimited sum — the actual figure was unimportant. To prevent the loss of another aircraft, some millions of dollars could be spent with the full support of the airline companies and the general public.

'And so,' Macklin concluded, 'I once

again move that this meeting sanction the immediate formation of the project that Mr. Ward and Miss Varick have proposed.'

As if by prior arrangement, with perfect timing, a discreet knock on the door heralded the entry of two smart uniformed girls carrying trays of coffee and biscuits.

Many delegates stood up to stretch their legs, taking the opportunity to chat informally amongst themselves. A small crowd gathered around Ward.

Dr. Bateman, who had flown from Washington where he was responsible for studies into U.F.O. activity on behalf of the U.S. Government, was anxious to have a private word with the Englishman.

'Mr. Ward,' he said, 'may I ask you if establishing a common pattern of preceding events will allow you to predict an accident that may take place in the future?'

Ward felt a sudden increase in the pressure of Joanne's hand against his leg where she was standing beside him.

'Yes of course you can ask me that,' he replied easily, 'the answer — as I'm sure you know already — is simply that it depends entirely on the type of pattern that is discovered. If we're lucky and it's a straightforward one — like equipment malfunction or maybe the fact that our charming Arab friends have again been waging their own highly individualistic crusade against airline passengers of a certain nationality — then accurate predictions are not difficult to make. In this case though, we'll never be able to check them — the sacrifice of another aircraft full of innocent people just to prove a theory would not be permitted by Miss Varick I'm afraid.'

Bateman scowled at the younger man. 'Do you find the death of some hundreds of passengers amusing to contemplate?'

'No — do you?'

'You were making the joke.'

Ward shrugged. 'If you allow the tragedy of the thing to get through to you the job will suffer — ask any doctor or nurse in a casualty ward.'

'It will take too long your way and your chances of success are poor,' Bateman said, 'and we may not have much time. I still think that a complete sonar sweep along the flight paths would be a more positive approach and yield answers more quickly.'

One of the representatives from Military Intelligence — Colonel Ralph Douglas — joined the conversation. 'The Pacific is extremely deep and a very large place, Doctor Bateman, a search for sunken wreckage is one hell of a job. You might stand a chance with supersensitive oil detectors and then compute drifts to pinpoint the source, but it's too late for that, even for the last one that went down.'

Bateman said, 'P.Y.432 is on the bottom somewhere out there,' he waved his hand at the window. 'I still believe we can find it.'

'How do you know it's on the bottom?' Ward asked.

'Where else would it be? Sure it might be in bits but they'll be on the bottom too.'

Ward grinned at him. 'You're the U.F.O. man — for all we know it might have gone straight up.'

The doctor turned his back and walked away. At the same time, Macklin was calling for order, announcing that the meeting would resume at once.

'Keep at them, Chris,' Joanne whispered as she left to return to her seat. Ward felt the closeness that had been developing between them was progressing nicely. He again began to wonder how she felt about him.

When the coughing and the shuffling of papers had died down, the Colonel from the Intelligence Department indicated to Macklin that he wished to speak.

'Miss Varick,' he nodded graciously to her, 'and gentlemen — before our coffee, Mr. Ward urged us to come to a decision. I should like to align myself with the sentiments he expressed and propose a formal motion to accept the suggestion which he has made to this assembly.

'The formation of a project team to undertake a statistical analysis of every facet of these disasters can be sanctioned by this meeting immediately. Such a move does not prevent us from also deciding to carry out a full sonar survey of the ocean bed in selected areas — nor does it prevent us from launching a project to see if oil leaks from sunken aircraft can be detected by using some of the modern equipment which has been described to us today.

'Of course there are doubts as to the success of these ventures — that does not mean they are worthless. Let us adopt all of them — God knows there is too much at stake to place all of our eggs in one basket.'

One of the men from Flight Security felt that his suggestion had been omitted from the list of projects.

He said, 'And what about satellite radar reconnaissance?'

Macklin and Douglas answered together, both agreeing that the method should be formally adopted together with the others that had been mentioned.

The tone of the meeting had improved, members now no longer competing against each other with their ideas but instead, talking excitedly about the possibilities of techniques proposed by other delegates.

Ward sat back comfortably in his chair, knowing that he could look forward to establishing his own project in which pretty Joanne Varick would take a vital position. All he had to do now was to recruit his support staff and decide upon the location of the base from which he would operate. He listened to Macklin's summary of the decisions, hearing himself named as project co-ordinator for the analysis group, but not bothering to take notes or absorb much of the detail that delegates were beginning to discuss. Instead, Ward allowed himself the luxury of studying Joanne.

Choosing to complete their business at one sitting, lunch was delayed until just after two o'clock.

Eating their meal in the plush dining room of the I.A.S. building, Ward and Joanne Varick debated the initial steps that would have to be taken before their work could begin properly.

Just before the coffee was served, Ward switched off.

'Miss Varick,' he said, deliberately avoiding the use of her Christian name.

'I thought we agreed it was Joanne some weeks ago,' she said, smiling at his artificially serious expression.

'Miss Varick,' he repeated, 'for nearly two weeks we have been working to produce a concrete proposal for this morning's meeting. When we haven't been doing that, we have been attending lectures on the procedures used to screen airline passengers, lectures on how to fly aircraft and lectures on how to land aircraft. Our heads have been filled with the awful fact that over five hundred ordinary people have failed to reach their destinations after entrusting their money and their lives to four major airline companies. I have had enough, Miss Varick — for just a while I have had enough.

'This afternoon and for far into the night I am going to relax. As you are to report to me on this assignment, you will of course do precisely as I say and on this occasion I am instructing you to accompany me as I relax — do you understand?'

She nodded. 'Yes, Mr. Ward.'

'Not Mr. Ward — sir.'

'Yes, sir.'

'Are you ready, Miss Varick?'

'No, I haven't finished my coffee.'

'Drink it.'

'It's too hot, Chris.'

'I can't help that — drink it.'

Minutes later they walked out into George Street, the heat and exhaust fumes of central Sydney seeming unbearable after the conditioned air inside the building.

'I thought the air-conditioning wasn't any good in there?' Ward said, wiping beads of perspiration from his forehead.

'Would you rather be back in London — remember the paper said it was the coldest January for eight years there?'

'No — this'll do fine thanks — ' Ward turned to look at his assistant.

Joanne Varick was twenty three, five feet six inches tall with a good figure and her face and arms were already tanned from the short period of exposure to the Australian sunshine. Short blonde hair curled around her rather round face, reducing the otherwise startling effect of her hazel coloured eyes. She looked smart in her sleeveless cotton dress and very desirable.

'Where are you going to relax?' she asked, returning Ward's critical stare.

'Manley beach — big Manley.'

'You're mad — how are you going to relax with all those people?'

Ward flagged a yellow Holden taxi, holding open the door for Joanne to climb in.

'Your legs are getting brown too,' he observed, conducting careful examination before shutting the door.

The driver waited patiently for directions.

'Around Sydney — the usual things — the opera house of course, the bridge and then Manley,' Ward instructed.

Being an intimate part of Sydney's traffic problem proved much less exhausting than observing it as a pedestrian and the temperature inside the car soon reduced with forward motion.

Joanne smiled at Ward where he had collapsed in the corner of the back seat, the corners of her mouth puckering slightly.

'You're not relaxed,' she said, 'you're pretending aren't you?'

'A bit,' he admitted.

'I've seen you relax before, Chris — what's bothering you?'

Ward shook his head slowly. 'Two things, Miss Varick. Firstly, I have a firm rule that says that thou shalt not embark upon any project with preconceived ideas — ' his voice tailed away.

'And the other thing?'

'You.'

'What?'

He lifted a hand a few inches from the seat. 'I wasn't going to say anything,' he said.

There was a pause before she answered him. 'I'm not sure I know what you mean but if it's nothing to do with work but is about you and me — then I feel just the same way, Chris.'

Knowing she had made a mess of what was supposed to have been a carefully worded reply, she coloured, dropping her eyes immediately from his face.

But enough had been said by both of them and seconds later she was in his arms, yielding to a desire that had been suppressed too long.

With customary tact, the driver deflected his rear view mirror, concentrating on his unequal battle against the afternoon traffic.

3

Two miles south of Los Angeles International air terminal, a curious mixture of urban development and modern light industry has sprawled across part of the city. Offices of major aircraft manufacturing companies rub shoulders with equally tall and equally pretentious motel buildings and everywhere, penetrating every room, every street and every car, there is the roar of big jets as they thunder day and night along the tarmac strips. The acrid stench of burnt aviation fuel hangs heavily in the already overladen air, whilst the thin evil blanket of the ever present smog dims the otherwise magnificent sight of distant mountains.

But the companies who have established their headquarters in this place and the people who work in the offices are not there to enjoy the view. It is the convenience of the area, the association with L.A. International and L.A. Domestic that has caused the area to grow in such a peculiar way.

Executives can commute from Pomona, from Ventura or from Santa Barbara with effortless ease, their journeys terminating with the short helicopter flight to the roofs of the buildings in which they work. Visitors from any State of the Union and visitors from overseas can be accommodated in the numerous hotels and motels that have been established in the area without having to travel great distances to the board rooms of nearby companies. The entire area is widely regarded by the people who work there as most convenient — to be there for any other purpose is an extremely unpleasant experience.

Christopher Ward had chosen to locate his enterprise here for no other reason than expediency. On two floors of a large building owned by the El Segundo Aircraft Equipment Organisation, project P.D.3. had crammed over thirty people, two digital computers with enlarged store capacities and a communication system of incredible complexity.

Only in the United States could a project of this nature be established so quickly and with such little effort. Australia, New Zealand and Polynesia, whilst closer to the suspected areas of the four inexplicable air disasters, could not hope to match the facilities that the west coast of America could provide and, before Ward had left Australia, he had known that the mighty Californian city of Los Angeles was the best place from which to carry out his plans.

This morning, Christopher Ward was tired, partly as the result of overwork and partly from mixing his work with a heavy overdose of Joanne Varick the night before.

The six telephones on his desk remained silent as he watched two antacid tablets fizz in a glass of water. Joanne entered the room as he was drinking.

'Good morning, Miss Varick.'

She stood on tip toe to kiss him, noticing the slight fatigue in his eyes. 'You're tired, Chris — how about easing up today?'

'What do you want me to ease up on — P.D.3.?'

P.D.3 stood for Pacific disaster investigation team three, a programme that had been in full operation now for nearly a month. Yesterday, the first real results of Joanne's computer run had caused a minor sensation amongst the senior members of the project, culminating in a private celebration lasting well into the night at the nearby hotel where most of them were staying.

Ward unwound Joanne's arms from his neck. 'Okay,' he said, 'but first we review what we think is a breakthrough just to make sure it is a breakthrough.'

He withdrew a large tape recorder from the top drawer of his filing cabinet and placed it on the desk, waiting for Joanne to reappear with the computer documents and the summary of them that the analysts had compiled.

'What about Steven and Graham Redlands,' she asked from the door, 'don't you want them?'

'They're busy on phase three now and we don't need them for a review

— just you and I, Jo.'

She sat down to face him across the desk. 'I can't get used to this double life, Chris — we'd work better if we hated each other.'

He nodded. 'I know but there's nothing we can do about it now — I can't manage without you — on the project I mean — ' he grinned briefly, 'and there's too much at stake and too much still left to be done for me to resign. Anyway, I think we might just be close to cracking the problem — then we can do what the hell we like without having the damned importance of the job hanging over us all the time.'

'I haven't noticed it inhibiting you.'

'Shut up, Miss Varick, and let's get going on the review. I'll tape the whole thing and someone can type an edited report from it afterwards.'

Ward flipped the switch to disconnect his telephones and pushed the red button on the tape recorder.

'Christopher Ward and Joanne Varick of P.D.3 in Los Angeles on February the twentieth,' he said into the double sided

46

microphone, 'this tape should be filed in S.9 and will form the basis for a summary on the work leading to our conclusions on the significance of the Met. and Passenger Record levels.'

For the remainder of the morning the spools on the recorder turned as the two people reviewed the work that P.D.3 had accomplished. In such a short time a staggering quantity of data had been examined and sifted.

Once sufficient staff had been recruited, the project had been split into data gathering groups under the leadership of selected experts. All of the information was fed into the computers where it was stored for the purpose of future comparison, four separate stores being compiled, one for each of the aircraft that had disappeared.

Flight T.P.308, a Trans Pacific Airline D.C.8 from San Francisco to Nandi was the first. Approximately half way to Fiji, contact had been lost with the aircraft and on June the thirteenth the search had been called off. No explanation for the tragedy had ever been found.

47

In August, a 707 of French International, en route from Noumea to Suva, failed to arrive on schedule although immediate checks showed that it had departed on time. F.I.003 was never seen again.

Then — and it was Flight A.A.961 that removed all thoughts of coincidence from the minds of Air Security — a new D.C.10 of AustralAmerican disappeared somewhere on the long trip from Sydney to San Diego. Mercifully the jumbo was flying on an unpopular route and less than half full but twenty seven children had been on board the fated plane. A.A.961 was listed as officially missing only five weeks after the French International disaster.

P.Y.432 in December had frightened public and airlines alike, the shipping companies receiving a most unexpected and welcome boost in passenger trade. Massive, though unco-ordinated, attempts to discover the cause of the disasters had revealed nothing and it was this failure that had prompted the meeting in Sydney just over four weeks ago. Since then, the

P.D.3 team had done little but accumulate data — nearly two tons of it, all sifted now and safe in the computer storage systems. Waste paper disposal had been just one of the minor problems of P.D.3.

Information associated with the disasters was categorised, the number of separate classification headings being kept to a minimum although they now ran into several hundreds. It was for this reason that computer techniques offered the only practical solution to the problem of correlating data.

Apart from conventional information on passengers such as sex, nationality, age, marital status, height, weight and other statistics, a file of minute detail on each person was painstakingly composed including almost every individual characteristic that could possibly be discovered. Relatives, frequently still grief stricken, were questioned about the personal habits of their late wives or husbands or brothers. Mothers were asked to provide details on the marriages of their sons and daughters — were they happy unions? — was there hate in the family? — had there been a record of insanity? It was a sickening business, calling for a particular investigating skill that was not easily learnt. The telephone bill for P.D.3 exceeded fifteen thousand dollars for the first twenty six days of its operation.

In equal detail, the histories of each aircraft were studied, a different kind of investigator being needed for this highly technical exercise. Airframe stresses that were known to be near maximum safe limits were obtained from manufacturers and an extensive examination of the mock-ups that were under continual simulated stress in test complexes across the United States provided yet more data to be stored. The histories of each engine on each of the four aircraft were studied, the maintenance sheets from service departments providing a wealth of complicated information that required interpretation by qualified engineers.

Meteorological reports for the days on which the aircraft crashed were broken down into fine detail. Readings of temperature, pressure, humidity, sea conditions and a host of other scientific data covering the behaviour of the ocean and the atmosphere were fed into the vast memory banks of the computers. Satellite photographs of the cloud formations were compared using optical scanning heads connected through interface units to the expensive computing machines that were the tools of P.D.3.

The defence departments of co-operating nations or their governments were asked to supply reports on the movement of military aircraft, surface craft or submarines that were operating in what were believed to be the accident areas on the dates of the crashes. Girls who had sold tickets to the passengers that had perished in the disasters were interviewed, people who had cancelled reservations were questioned about their reasons and the maintenance crews that had serviced the aircraft for the last fateful flights were asked to submit reports on airworthiness. P.D.3 was a colossal enterprise. Only someone of Ward's ability could ever have controlled it.

As they summarised the gathering

phase of the project, speaking slowly to each other and into the impersonal grille of the microphone, both Ward and Joanne began to realise how much ground had been covered in such a relatively short period of time.

The principal reason for producing a taped summary at this stage of their investigation was the fact that Joanne had been able to supply evidence showing that the weather conditions existing along the flight routes had been similar for each accident. There was more significance attached to this simple discovery than might be supposed. Whilst the Pacific ocean is widely regarded as a placid body of water, apart from the occasional tropical cyclones that move southwards in the warmer months, there are neverthe-less quite large changes in surface conditions and even larger day to day alterations in the upper atmosphere. In the computers, the meteorological infor-mation had been compared for each of the days on which the four aircraft had disappeared and the resultant pattern had in turn been similarly compared with the average weather pattern that should exist in the crash zones. For the first time an astounding and precise similarity was observed.

The result was even more remarkable for the comparitive rareness of the weather type that apparently had attended the disasters. When T.P.308, F.I.003, A.A.961 and P.Y.432 had lost contact with the world, the weather had been so exceptionally tranquil that similar conditions could be expected statistically for less than one per cent of the year. In round figures, for only three days in each year would the weather be as calm as it was when the aircraft had vanished. P.D.3 had established the first vital link in the chain.

Ward switched off the tape recorder for a moment and stood up.

'It's interesting,' he said, 'but it doesn't mean a damn thing by itself.'

'When we find a few more facts it will,' Joanne answered, letting a sheaf of folded computer print-outs cascade to the floor.

'How many similarities do you think we'll find?' Ward asked.

'The more we find the easier it should

be to pinpoint a cause but we could get so many that significance of each one becomes doubtful — we'll just have to carry on and see — I don't know how many more we'll discover.'

Ward walked round the desk to stand beside her.

'But why good weather — excellent weather — what the hell would make an aircraft crash in such perfect conditions?'

'Wait and see — we'll find out.'

'When is your next computer run?'

'Monday — we're not working this weekend, remember?'

Ward grinned at her, 'I could insist you stay here and I'll go to the cabin myself.'

'Suit yourself — have a good time.'

'I'll take that little programmer from along the corridor — the one with the nice legs and glasses.'

Joanne stood up and stretched. 'You'd be bored with her by Saturday night,' she said confidently.

'But not with you?'

She snuggled up to Ward's lean body. 'I haven't bored you so far have I Mr. Clever Project Leader?'

'No — I don't think you ever will.'

Ward responded to her embrace pushing her backwards to the edge of the table.

'Chris?'

'Mmm.'

'The summary tape — we haven't covered the passenger analysis yet.'

He released her, straightened his tie and returned to his swivel chair.

'Okay career girl,' he said smiling at his assistant, 'let's go.'

She bit back her answer, knowing he had switched on the recorder again hoping that she hadn't noticed.

'Do you want to change straight to the passenger records?' she asked primly.

'Yes please.'

Joanne opened the blue file containing the results from the computer comparison that had taken so much work to produce. She flipped over the pages of distribution graphs. Each of the aircraft had contained an average number of women, an average number of men, an average number of children.

The results of the analysis showed a

depressingly normal distribution of people. Not only were there exactly the right number of divorced women to satisfy the statistical norm but each of the aircraft had contained precisely the correct number of Polynesian male children under the age of three. There were some deviations, especially in the case of the relatively empty D.C.10, but none of them were of great significance. Only in one tiny area was there a glimmer of something unusual.

Distribution theory showed that a small — a very small — proportion of the passengers would have a criminal record, or be suspected but not convicted of criminal activity. The classifications were broad — violence, theft, sexual assault, drugs and miscellaneous. It was in the drug category that an irritatingly small deviation from the normal distribution had been detected by the computer making it difficult for the analysts to decide on the significance level. In two of the flights there had been men suspected of drug trafficking, but the information that the International Drug Squad had supplied was based on doubtful suspicions and there was no rapid way to improve upon the quality of their evidence.

Ward and Joanne spent some time discussing the validity of their conclusions knowing that the tape recording would be used only to form the basis of a report. In the end, Ward decided that their doubts would be best kept to themselves and that P.D.3 should issue a formal and positive announcement. By attaching a low level of significance to the discovery it was simple to make a clear statistical statement of fact without the need for any interpretation at this stage.

The remainder of the morning was employed in a brief review of the other analyses that Joanne had completed. None of them had produced conclusions so far, but much work was still to be done and it was much too early to be pessimistic.

Four hours had elapsed since they had started recording. Ward's throat was dry from talking.

'Lunch,' he announced switching off the recorder.

'One and a half more days,' she said, 'then two whole days to ourselves.'

Ward pulled her to her feet. 'Come on, Jo, I promised we'd have lunch with Graham.'

'Aren't you going to lock the tape up?'

'It'll be all right there until this afternoon.'

An hour later, when Ward returned to his office, he was mildly surprised to find the take off spool on the recorder not properly seated on its spindle. Thinking that his secretary must have disturbed it whilst clearing his desk top, he removed the tape from the machine and locked the magnetic record securely in his filing cabinet. Four days later Christopher Ward would remember the incident and regard it in a very different light.

*　*　*

Whilst the analysts of P.D.3 waited for their computers to disgorge still more

58

information, many thousands of miles away from Los Angeles in a far less polluted environment, the vessels of P.D.1 pushed on through the sparkling blue of the South Pacific.

Two Australian frigates, carrying crews of one hundred and eighty five men pursued the courses of T.P.308 and F.I.003, their sonar equipment scanning the deeps for any echo that would indicate the presence of a sunken aircraft. On each side of the hulls, water sampling equipment continually checked for faint traces of oil or fuel which might perhaps have escaped from ruptured tanks. The technique was not a success.

The crystal Pacific was by no means as clean as it appeared.

Each year, an estimated thirteen million tons of hydrocarbon products are deposited by man in the oceans of the world of which at least one tenth is oil. Spillage from tankers and oil rigs joins with ten million tons of gasoline which has evaporated to be eventually deposited in the sea. The sensitive oil detectors that the frigates carried proved beyond all doubt that the Pacific was awash with oil.

On board, scientists were kept busy in their makeshift laboratories as in vain they tried to separate the oils into categories that would allow them to isolate aircraft lubricants and fuels.

The sonar search was more positive but no encouraging echoes had yet been received and it was said that to undertake a comprehensive exploration of the ocean bed along the flight paths which the aircraft had followed would require many passes.

The routes of A.A.961 and P.Y.432 were being followed by two survey vessels, large ships of nearly three thousand tons loaned by the Pacific fleet of the United States. Apart from a few hours of excitement when the sonar of the vessel sailing from San Diego picked up definite echoes from what was rumoured to be a Soviet submarine, the voyages had so far yielded no information of direct use to P.D.1.

★　★　★

Since the disappearance of P.Y.432 in December, some airlines had discontinued all scheduled flights across the Pacific. Others, anxious to seize the opportunity to increase their profits, offered those passengers who were willing to take the risk a variety of new flights which avoided the well-publicised routes on which the disasters had occurred.

Throughout the world, public reaction had been astonishingly slight, the sensational treatment of the accidents in the newspapers and on television failing to surprise or move the ordinary man or woman. It is said that the same fifteen per cent of the population fill ninety per cent of each flight which, in part, was thought to explain what nearly amounted to disinterest amongst the bulk of the population. There were some people though, who were watching the progress of the Pacific Disaster Investigation teams with great interest; people unconnected with the airlines and not directly concerned with the loss of lives or the loss in revenue for the carriers. These were scientists — aware that four crashes in such a short period of time was a highly improbable statistic unless an outside element was at work. Men who, although not part of the P.D. teams, still maintained a keen interest in the reports that were issued periodically from the I.A.S. headquarters in Sydney. Some of them had seriously considered the possibility of interference in the routine flights by an extraterrestrial agent, but such notions were not widely publicised.

The periodic radar searches which the satellites were maintaining had revealed nothing. The technique would be of no value unless it were able to detect the presence of something in the vicinity of another aircraft prior to its disappearance and there were serious doubts about the economics of continuing the system, even on a sporadic or random basis.

All of the P.D. teams were fully operational, but none of them was yet able to shed any light at all on the mystery that was exercising so many clever minds.

4

The intensity of the rain was greater now, the noise of it on the corrugated iron roof of the barn almost drowning the angry buzz of the chain saw. Water from the numerous leaks in the ancient roof was soaking both Christopher Ward and the heap of wood he had sawn.

He cut the ignition, looking for somewhere dry to store the little two-stroke driven saw. Two days of solid rain had thoroughly saturated the earth floor of the barn and Ward decided that he had better take the machine back to the cabin with him.

Waiting in vain for the rain to abate, he sprinted the few yards to the single door of the cabin trusting he would not trip over a tree root in the dark.

Joanne lay on the sheepskin rug in front of a blazing fire.

'Where's the wood?' she asked sweetly,

ignoring Ward's dishevelled and water-logged appearance.

'I left it in the barn for you to fetch.'

'I am not wet and I am not covered in wood chips like you are — common logic says it would be better for you to get it.'

'What's it worth? — it's raining like hell out there and black as pitch.'

She waved a dainty foot at him, keeping the blue housecoat drawn modestly around her legs.

Ward slammed the door. A few minutes later he reappeared, staggering under an enormous load of damp fire wood.

'That should keep us going until we go to bed,' he said, shaking the rain from his hair.

'I ran a bath for you, Chris, and I put the wine in the fridge — don't be long, darling.'

Ward threw two logs onto the fire and retired to the bathroom.

Soaking in the warm water, he thought that it was going to be difficult to return to P.D.3. Two days here with Joanne had almost convinced him that the life of a gentleman backwoodsman had so much to commend it that any other career would seem dull in comparison.

They had driven up here to Devil's Canyon on Friday evening finding the vacation cabin which belonged to one of the aeronautical experts attached to P.D.3 with little difficulty despite the rain. Since their arrival the weather had stubbornly refused to improve and their time had been spent almost entirely indoors. Not that it had mattered Ward thought — both of them had been able to unwind, forgetting the project and talking about themselves instead.

Joanne Varick had shown herself to be an excellent cook, the pair of them spending the two days in splendid self-indulgence leaving the comfortable cabin only to fetch wood for the open fire and to collect more provisions from the car. Isolated from civilisation, far from the noise and stink of Los Angeles, Ward and Joanne had experienced little trouble in ridding themselves of the pressures of their work. Now it was Sunday night and Ward knew that in a few more hours he would again have to assume the responsibilities of being the co-ordinator of P.D.3.

He climbed from the bath, dried himself and dressed. Joanne was waiting for him in the lounge — Ward allowed sweet anticipation to course through him making his skin tingle.

He collected two bottles of their favourite white wine from the refrigerator and walked into the warmth of the room.

'Hi,' she said.

Ward sat down beside her on the rug, gazing into the flames.

'Do you suppose it would be like this all the time if we were married?' he said.

'No, I don't think it would — we'd both change — we'd have to, but that doesn't mean it would lose everything. Things would just be different — but just as nice.'

'Do you think we should try, Jo?' he said suddenly.

Her reply was cut short by the faint noise of an engine, sounding as though a car was climbing the winding dirt road to the cabin.

'Who the hell could that be?' Ward said,

his mood abruptly changed.

'It must be someone from the project — no one else knows we're here,' Joanne answered. 'Perhaps they've got some urgent news?'

Ward shook his head, 'They know we'll be back tomorrow and it's a long drive from L.A. on a lousy night like this.'

The car was closer now.

'Are there any other cabins further on up the road, Chris?'

'Oh yes — they wouldn't build an expensive road like this for one holiday cottage — but who would be arriving on a Sunday night in February?'

Joanne stood up. 'I bet it's someone from the office.'

Gravel crunched under wet tyres outside the door, the headlights of the car shining through the curtains of the single window.

'It's for us all right,' Ward said, 'damn their eyes.'

He went to the door and opened it, peering into the rain.

With great violence the partly opened door was slammed into his face making him reel backwards into the room.

Four men entered, closing the door behind them. Uniformly dressed in black leather jackets and jeans, they were under thirty, unshaven and frightening. Each of them carried an axe handle.

White and terrified, with her hand over her mouth to stifle a scream, Joanne Varick stood on the rug unable to move.

Ward's throat was dry. He had regained his balance quickly and spun round to face the intruders, noticing the unintelligent coarse features and dirty long hair.

'What the hell do you think you're doing?' he said, the authority in his voice surprising him.

He received no answer, they were standing looking at the casually dressed girl, their hungry eyes making their intentions painfully clear.

'Chris,' Joanne whispered.

'Never mind him, baby — you have us now,' — one of the men spoke shortly.

Another reached out an axe handle to lift the hem of Joanne's house coat. She backed away, raw fear showing in her wide eyes.

Ward moved towards her knowing that he had more trouble on his hands than he had ever experienced in his life before. There was no time to think of why — right now, in this room, Christopher Ward had to make quite sure that he made no mistakes at all.

Warily, he continued to walk to the fireplace — but he stood no chance. Joanne's scream tore through Ward's head as two of the men wheeled in unison, their weapons swinging in wide arcs.

The first caught him on the left forearm as he tried to fend off the vicious blow. A fraction of a second later the other sank deeply into his side. Paralysed with the spreading agony, Ward sank to his knees gasping, unable to breathe and knowing he had failed.

The four moved closer to the girl forcing her backwards until the heat of the fire made further retreat impossible.

Utterly terrified, she held her hands in front of her as if to fend off the advancing men.

One of them roughly grasped her wrists pulling her towards him. 'Don't she smell nice,' he said to the others, 'all clean and fresh — she's gonna be something and I reckon she's all ready too.'

The smallest man of the group unbuttoned the house-coat pulling it back over the girl's shoulders. She wore matching bra and panties in a light coffee colour. Her entire body was shaking in fear.

On the floor, through a haze of pain, Ward watched helplessly. He was still alive and he was going to have to do something and he was going to have to do it now. Experimentally, still lying down, he flexed his limbs formulating his simple plan. Ward had squandered his first attempt — now, providing he could stand, there would be one more slender chance.

He counted slowly, trying to ignore Joanne's moans and then Ward made his move.

He was on his feet with the chain saw in his hands before the men could turn to meet him. Praying it would start, he pulled on the cord. There was a roar from the engine and Christopher Ward was armed with one of the most dangerous weapons that man had yet devised for hand to hand combat.

His head was relatively clear and although his entire side felt numb and weak, he could walk and move his arms.

Animal fear showed in the eyes of the intruders as they moved to surround him. One of them hesitated for a moment, then turned back to the girl.

Deliberately he swung the handle in a long sweeping arc lifting the tip upwards over Joanne's spread hands as she tried to defend herself. With a sickening crack the wooden haft caught her above the ear, splitting the skin in a long red line under the blonde hair. Her slight figure crumpled at once.

Ward shouted at the top of his voice and leapt forward opening the throttle on the saw to its maximum.

The axe handles were more manoeuvrable and their reach was nearly double that of the saw blade. Weaving and darting, his strength seeming to return with every second, Ward endeavoured to take each blow on the whirling chain. Contacting the serrated teeth the handles were wrenched violently in the hands of the four men, disturbing their balance and making them vulnerable to Ward's sudden dangerous thrusts.

The dull red haze of pain had vanished now. Joanne was dead, murdered in cold blood by these brutal men. An icy calm seized Ward, somehow making the attacks of his antagonists appear ineffective and slow.

Mercilessly he moved forward into closer combat, dodging the wild swings of the axe handles or taking them deliberately on the saw.

Then, with the shriek of the motor echoing in his ears, Ward made a sudden vicious thrust with the tip of the saw. Effortlessly, the wicked teeth tore a long bloody slot in the chest of the man to Ward's left. Blood sprayed out from the chain saw leaving a thin line along the ceiling and the floor.

Seconds later Ward laid open the right shoulder of another of them, the bone shining white in the firelight.

He had done enough. Leaving one of their number dead upon the cabin floor the others bolted for the door, the man with the gaping wound in his shoulder sobbing in pain. Ward let them go.

Trembling uncontrollably from a dreadful combination of pain, fear and exhaustion, he throttled back the engine of the saw and turned it off. Through the window he watched the dim shape of the car leave the clearing outside the cabin, its outline being obscured by sheets of rain before it reached the open gate.

He listened until he could hear the sound of the car no more, then, after bolting the door, he went to attend to Joanne.

Parts of the floor were awash with frothy blood and the room was filled with exhaust fumes from the chain saw. In the flickering firelight, with the body of the dead man sprawled grotesquely across part of the rug, a nightmarish scene confronted Ward. The girl lay still, her figure twisted upon the soft blue house-coat.

Fighting the pain in his side he knelt down to lift the wrist of the girl, knowing that the terrible blow she had suffered must have killed her instantaneously. But there was a faint pulse there, weak and irregular but a definite gentle pumping.

Almost unable to believe that Joanne could still be alive, frantically Ward placed his head on her cool moist skin to listen to her heart.

'Oh God,' he breathed softly, 'please God keep her alive for me.'

Gasping from the pain that felt as though his chest was being penetrated by knives of red hot steel, he wrapped the limp figure in the house-coat, struggling to make sure that he did not subject Joanne to any unnecessary movement.

With extreme difficulty, knowing that it was vital for him to retain consciousness, Ward carried the girl to his car, returning to the cabin almost as an afterthought to retrieve the blood spattered chain saw.

Knowing that there was a remote possibility of being ambushed on the only road leading from the cabin to Highway Two, he locked the car doors from the inside once he had arranged Joanne's loose-limbed body on the back seat.

He started the engine, turned on the

headlights and drove into the rain-streaked night leaving the horror of the cabin behind him.

Half an hour later, his reserves nearly exhausted, Ward drove through the wrought-iron gates of a large homestead, the first welcome lights of civilisation that he had seen marginally reviving his shocked system.

Without knowing whether or not Joanne was still alive, he staggered to the front door.

The elderly owner of the ranch was about to retire for the night when the doorbell rang. Being a practical man and aware of the dangers of opening his door to a stranger so late at night, he collected his shotgun from the den before investigating further.

Leaving the chain in the slot he pulled open the door, simultaneously switching on the porch light.

Leaning against the wall, bloodstained and wet, his eyes glazed, Ward was unable to speak. Hanging loosely in his hand the chain saw dripped blood on to the tiled floor.

Immediate efforts on the part of the startled owner of the house assisted by his wife and younger sister failed to induce Ward indoors. Eventually, summoning the dregs of fading energy that he thought had deserted him long ago, Ward managed to speak.

'Girl in the car — you must get Joanne to hospital — doctor — you must at once — please at once.'

The effort proved too much. Christopher Ward collapsed gracefully in the porch, his right hand still clutching the chain saw that had served him so well on this fateful night.

5

'Don't be so damn pessimistic,' Colonel Douglas grunted, 'things like that always take a long time and you know it, Chris.'

Ward swung his legs from the edge of the hospital bed. 'It's difficult to explain how I feel about Miss Varick,' he said.

'Oh spare me, Christopher — do you think I wasn't your age once — you're upsidedown in love with Joanne — everyone on P.D.3 told me and even if they hadn't I would have known.'

Ward's eyes glittered briefly. 'It wasn't interfering with our work.'

'I didn't suppose for a moment that it was. You're both old enough and intelligent enough to keep your personal affairs to yourselves.'

Ward shook his head slightly. 'I'd sure as hell be able to work better from now on if I knew she was going to be all right — they said it could still be weeks before they can be certain. They won't even let me see her.'

Douglas knew it was useless to continue discussing the subject. Only time would tell if the doctors and surgeons at the military hospital in Pasadena could bring Joanne Varick out of the deep coma. He also knew that the quicker Christopher Ward was back in harness, the quicker he would accept the past. There was vital work to be completed on P.D.3 and only Ward could do it now that Joanne was no longer part of the project.

'You'll be back in L.A. tomorrow?' Douglas asked.

'I could've been working three days ago if they'd have let me out of here — you'd think that modern medicine could fix up a couple of cracked ribs overnight rather than in seven days or however long it is now.'

'Just remember how it felt when you were first admitted,' Douglas reminded him dryly. 'I seem to recall you were convinced of ruptured lungs and smashed kidneys.'

Ward jumped off the bed. 'Never mind that now, have you got any more news?'

'Not really — we're absolutely sure that both of you were supposed to have been killed and equally sure that your assailants were hired for the job. It's not difficult to find plenty of hoodlums in L.A. who would be willing to undertake that kind of work. All it requires is cash.'

'And how did they know where we were?' Ward asked.

'Someone in P.D.3.'

'Someone who doesn't want the project to succeed?'

'I told you that several days ago,' Douglas said. 'It's thrown a completely different light on the whole thing.'

'A crank?'

'Maybe.'

A nurse pushed her head round the door of the private ward. 'You're supposed to be resting, Mr. Ward.'

Ward mouthed a rude word to her and she disappeared grinning.

'You think that someone wants more air disasters to happen?' he said seriously. 'I don't believe anyone on the project would get a kick out of something like that.'

Douglas lit a cigarette. 'Whatever it is, or whoever it is, from now on I have total responsibility for the security of the project, which includes the security of all the staff. You run the technical side of it and I look after you.'

'Are you still watching Joanne?'

'Two guards, twenty four hours a day inside a military hospital — will that do you?'

Ward didn't answer, his mind returning transiently to the last day he had spent at the office. Moving forward in time he experienced the cold hollow feeling in his stomach as he recalled the weekend in the cabin.

'Ralph,' he said slowly, 'I don't think I'm ever going to get over the thing that happened up there.'

The older man flicked the ash from his cigarette.

'No,' he answered, 'it'll take some doing I expect, but in time it will seem less vivid to you.'

'I killed a man.'

'You should've killed all of them — never forget they were there to kill you.'

'We don't know that for sure, Ralph.'

'No one drives up a dead end road in Devil's Canyon on a rotten night hoping to find a party to gate-crash or a piece of tail — they knew who you were and where to find you. There was no reason for them just to beat you up so that you could provide a description of them and subsequently testify against them if they were caught. They were there to kill you, Chris, and you did a fine job. Now quit worrying about it — you've got P.D.3 to worry about and that's pretty important to lots of people.'

'And I've got Joanne to worry about.'

The Colonel sighed. 'Yes, I guess you have.' He stubbed out the cigarette and prepared himself to leave.

'There'll be a car for you in the morning,' he said, 'I'll see you at the office first thing — now rest like your nurse said.'

He smiled at Ward, thinking that the young Englishman would have made a fine American. 'So long, Chris.'

Bandaged from his arm pits to his waist, Ward climbed back onto the hospital bed to think but found that the recent days spent in thinking about the nightmare he had been through had dulled his brain. Someone else would have to find the explanation for the attempted murder at the cabin; Ward's job was to carry P.D.3 through to a satisfactory conclusion — or were the two connected as Douglas believed? With the puzzle still revolving in his head, Ward fell asleep.

* * *

Several changes had been made to the El Segundo Aircraft Equipment building in the week that Ward had spent in hospital. The place was crawling with security guards.

A serious young American with a severe crew cut had accompanied Ward in the car on this bright sunny morning. Since introducing himself by means of an identification card that stated his name was Glen Yesler and that he worked for Military Intelligence, he had avoided all Ward's attempts to prompt conversation, his answers being polite but unimaginative.

When the car drew up outside the entrance leading to the offices of P.D.3, Yesler sprang out to hold open the car door for Ward.

'Thank you,' Ward said curtly, 'but you don't have to do things like that for me — I'm not used to it and I don't like it.'

Unperturbed, Yesler escorted Ward inside the building. Douglas was waiting for them in the small room at the top of the stairs.

'Good to see you here, Chris,' he said, handing Ward a plastic identification card. 'Wear this all the time you're here please — and no arguments.'

Ward pinned it to the lapel of his jacket. 'I trust Mr. Yesler will not want to sit with me in my office,' he said.

Douglas grinned at him. 'No, and we'll let you go to the can by yourself too.'

'I'll be outside the door of your office, Mr. Ward, if you want me,' Yesler sounded slightly embarrassed.

'Wonderful,' Ward muttered, striding along the corridor nodding good mornings to the staff who were staring at him from the office doorways.

Mary Cawston, Ward's secretary, met him at the door to his own office. She thrust a cup of coffee at him and smiled brightly. 'Welcome home, chief — we missed you.'

She followed him in, closing the door in the face of Glen Yesler.

'How is she?' she asked.

'I don't know any more than you do, Mary — they won't let me see her. All I know is that she's still unconscious and that they don't know how long it'll take.'

'But she's going to be okay?'

'If she isn't I'll never be able to forgive myself.'

His secretary stared at him. 'Now you snap out of that,' she said sternly, 'I've heard all about it and everyone here is real proud of you. The project is a mess and with Joanne out of it you're going to have to run it by yourself — I am going to make sure you do run it and you won't be able to unless you quit worrying about Jo.'

Ward nodded at her knowing she was right. It would be easier once he started again.

'I've forgotten a lot in a week,' he said, 'I'll replay that tape we made and then perhaps you could type an interim summary report from it this afternoon.'

Mary Cawston unlocked the file and withdrew the spool. 'Hey, let me do that,' she said watching Ward lift the heavy tape recorder.

He ignored her. 'I have two cracked ribs which are healing well,' he said, 'you are not to treat me like an invalid.'

'Yes, chief' she said, trying to look prim.

'Now get the hell out of here,' Ward grinned, 'and coffee every hour — with biscuits.'

He threaded the tape and pushed the playback button waiting to hear his own voice and wondering how he was going to feel when Joanne spoke.

Ward waited. After a few moments his impatience got the better of him and he depressed the rapid play control. Twenty feet of tape sped through the machine, but still there was nothing. He increased the volume leaving the speed control on rapid, cursing the recorder for its refusal to operate correctly.

And then Ward stopped it, a nagging fear tugging at his brain.

Quickly he changed the mode to record. 'One, two, three,' he said into the tiny microphone that was built into the side of the base. Seconds later, the few feet of tape containing his simple message was re-reeled ready to play back.

Ward stood up to listen. With deliberation he placed a finger on the button and increased the pressure.

'One, two, three.'

Christopher Ward slumped back in his chair, sure now that his suspicions were confirmed.

'Mary,' he shouted, 'get Colonel Douglas and come in here.'

While he waited, Ward collected a pile of tapes from the file inspecting each one closely.

Mary Cawston and the Colonel entered

the room to find Ward's desk strewn with unwound lengths of magnetic tape.

'Ah,' Ward said, 'you're here.'

'What is it, Chris?' Douglas asked.

'We did a summary tape — Joanne and I — before the weekend. I remember leaving it on the recorder while we had lunch. When I got back here one of the spools had been disturbed but I thought nothing of it at the time.'

Ward lifted up the spool. 'I've just played it back — there's nothing on it.'

'You mean it's been wiped?' Douglas asked.

'That's what I thought but look — ' Ward thrust two clear plastic spools at him. 'The spool isn't the type that we normally use, the colour of the leader isn't the same and look carefully at the tape — the one in your left hand there.'

Mary Cawston inspected it closely together with the Colonel.

'It's brand new,' she said suddenly, 'no scratches — so is the spool. It's not one of ours, chief.'

'Exactly,' Ward agreed.

'A substitute,' Douglas said, 'a complete substitute — someone has got your summary and what it contained frightened them — you must have been getting warm, Chris. That's why they tried to — ' his voice trailed off.

'Yeah,' Ward said, 'I think so. But I remember just about all of that tape and all the records are still here — so am I.'

'Fingerprints,' Mary Cawston said.

Douglas nodded. 'It's worth a try — I'll arrange it straight away.'

There was a gleam in Ward's eyes. 'We're close, Mary — and Douglas must be right — someone doesn't want us to find out why those aircraft crashed.'

'That's crazy.'

'Perhaps — but all the pieces fit, don't they. I wonder how near the truth we are?'

Ward's brain was racing now, sifting through the results of the analyses that he had discussed with Joanne. The met data and the passenger criminal records must somehow be more important than he had thought they were.

'I'll be with Colonel Douglas,' he said,

'don't let anyone in here without the permission of Mr. Yesler and don't you touch anything.'

He spoke briefly to the man from Military Intelligence who stood outside the door and walked rapidly along the corridor to the Colonel's new office.

'Do you believe me now?' Douglas asked him.

'I can't think of any other explanation, Ralph.'

Douglas pointed a finger. 'Someone in P.D.3 changed tapes during the time you were out of the office. Whoever it is knows just how far P.D.3 has got with its analysis and they want to stop it from proceeding any further. They've tried to kill you once — they might have another try.'

'We can prevent that easily.'

'How?'

'By making public all of our information — Joanne and I won't be special then.'

The Colonel looked at the co-ordinator of P.D.3 with despair. 'Don't be so bloody stupid,' he said, 'you're valuable because of what you can do with statistics and correlation theory, not because of what you know or what you've discovered so far.'

'Joanne is the correlation expert, not me.'

'I know that, but you're just as vital — you know what I mean.'

Douglas placed the palms of his hands on the blotter. 'As for making the information public — I have a feeling that would be unwise.'

'I suppose you already know what that tape covered,' Ward said.

'Exceptionally calm weather in the crash zones and an incredibly small deviation from the normal level in the criminal passenger records — in the drug category, I believe.'

'And you don't think that should be made public?' Ward asked.

'No.'

The telephone on the desk rang. Douglas listened for a few moments.

'So what,' he said sharply into the receiver, 'that doesn't tell me anything — a motive, man — a motive.' He slammed down the instrument.

'Fools,' he said, 'the car that carried those thugs to your cabin was stolen from Culver City. It's taken them a whole week to find that out.'

Ward wasn't listening. A fantastic theory was forming in his imaginative brain, a theory which had not before occurred to Christopher Ward and one that he was almost unwilling to conceive. But he could not stop it.

Douglas was still talking as if far away, Ward's mind blanking out all unnecessary external communication.

'My God,' Ward said finally.

The Colonel said 'What?' — surprised at the expression on Ward's face.

It was the sudden flash of inspiration that set Ward apart from the other men educated in the disciplines of science and mathematics; moments like the one he had just experienced had made it possible for Christopher Ward to command respect amongst his contemporaries and to lead teams of highly trained experts. Ward had just earned his not inconsiderable salary for several years.

Wondering if the Colonel had experienced a similar thought, Ward approached the subject gently.

'I'm sorry,' he said, 'I was thinking aloud. You were saying you believe we shouldn't make our findings public.'

Ward's curiosity was unfounded. A solid and intelligent man the Colonel, but not blessed with great originality of thought.

'Because you are spending vast quantities of dollars on a project which the general public will not understand — if anyone equates the results of your enquiry with the money spent, there'll be a public outcry that we'll never stop. People can understand sonar searches but not statistics, Chris. When you've discovered the answer — then we can crow and nobody will care how much it has cost.'

Very slowly and with care Ward said, 'I think I have the answer already — a horrible and evil answer. Only you and I are going to know about it, Ralph — nobody else — not yet anyway. If I'm right and this grotesque idea of mine is right, one of the most diabolic schemes that the civilised world has ever known is at work in our midst right now.'

Douglas went to the door and locked it.

'Okay,' he said, 'let's hear it, Mr. Ward.'

'It's only a wild idea.'

'You have a reputation for wild ideas that turn out to be pretty close to the truth,' Douglas said dryly. 'Anyway you started off by saying you thought you had the answer — stop back pedalling and unload it.'

'Okay, Colonel — try this then. That tape only contained two real pieces of information — the rest of it was just a lot of words. Whoever stole that tape could not have obtained anything of any importance from it except our conclusions and one of those was based on doubtful evidence. Now it seems that the met data and the passenger criminal record study have frightened someone enough to force them to make an attempt to kill us — it follows therefore, that the data must be of critical importance.

'Using these few facts it is not difficult to think of a situation which would explain the whole thing.'

'What?' Douglas said, frustrated at the slow approach of the younger man.

'Those aircraft didn't crash accidentally, Ralph — it was deliberate — deliberate mass murder of hundreds of people.'

A peculiar expression flitted across the Colonel's face. He said nothing.

Ward continued. 'Somehow or other, exceptionally fine weather is necessary for the operation and I bet you a million dollars there is only one explanation for slaughter on such a scale — money — enormous profits. And where do you find profits large enough to justify killing on these proportions in this day and age? — Drugs!'

'Good God!' Douglas said, 'it can't be true.'

'I hope it isn't but it fits well doesn't it?'

'Do you think they've been shot down, Chris?'

'I haven't the faintest idea, but I doubt it — the captains would have had time to radio a message unless they shot the front of the planes off first. More likely someone with a gun inside.'

Douglas shook his head. 'You can't

bring down a jet aircraft on the Pacific and hope to get away with it — anyone inside would have to face at least a ten per cent chance of dying when the plane hit the water.'

'Okay,' Ward countered, 'bombs — timed to explode at the right moment.'

'How does your drug theory fit that — why blow up a plane in mid air if you're in the drug business? What good is that going to do?'

'I don't know, but sure as hell I'm going to find out.'

Both men stared at each other trying to extend Ward's startling hypothesis and attempting to come to terms with the idea that the four air disasters had been deliberately planned.

Douglas broke the silence first. 'It's inconceivable,' he said, 'not with all those people on the aircraft — nobody could do such a thing.'

'Rubbish,' Ward replied callously, 'look at the records from the two world wars — one man in every thousand has no trouble in organising a massacre — some enjoy it and plenty of people think nothing of killing a few hundred people if the money is good enough.'

'You think one person is responsible?'

'No, I should think it's an organisation — a big one.'

'But you don't know?'

'How the hell could I? It's just an idea — I told you that — I might be way off the track — ' Ward sounded annoyed.

'It's a pretty terrible idea, Chris.'

'A week ago Joanne and I had a terrible experience, maybe it twisted my mind a little.'

'How easy is it going to be to check it out?' Douglas asked, lighting a cigarette and blowing a thin column of smoke into the air.

'Well, we can narrow our approach on P.D.3 and concentrate on the data that is directly relevant to my theory. Unfortunately, if I'm wrong, we might waste an awful lot of time.'

'Can you keep it to yourself?'

'For a while, I suppose, but there are some clever people here — it won't take them long to see where we're going. Anyway, if I'm right, someone here in this building already knows we're too close for comfort — remember you said the raid on the cabin must have originated here — it's obvious I suppose. Perhaps we've already done enough to make them realise that we'll catch up with them in the end — in fact I doubt if there'll be any more accidents now.'

For the remainder of the day they stayed behind locked doors in the Colonel's office, having Mary Cawston bring them lunch and the numerous cups of coffee without which Christopher Ward was unable to work.

Far reaching decisions were made that day, decisions that could have vindicated Ward's belief that P.D.3 would provide an answer to the air disasters. In a few more weeks, but for a handful of influential and narrow minded men who were unable to comprehend the power of modern statistics, P.D.3 would have been able to explain everything.

But it was not to be so.

Eleven days after Ward had first propounded his sinister theory, another aircraft disappeared.

6

The lights of Pasadena glittered brightly at him through the Californian night. Down there somewhere, Ward brooded, a hundred and twenty thousand people were going about their business, trusting that the organisations they had created to protect themselves were operating efficiently. To guard against the mugger, the rapist, the intruder and the psychopath there were the law enforcement agencies and to keep the United States free from attack by hostile foreign powers, the Department of Defence was spending billions of dollars on weapon systems. In the air space above this great continent and along the internationally agreed flight paths of the world, International Air Security maintained its vigil, watching for anything that might in any way usurp the inalienable right of the common man to travel safely by modern air transport. After overcoming the almost insurmountable problem of hijacking in the early seventies, I.A.S. was floundering now in its attempts to make safe the routes across the South Pacific.

It was not surprising, Ward thought ruefully — whilst the public might not be particularly disturbed — the chiefs of I.A.S. had a right to expect some sort of an answer from the millions of dollars that they had spent on the P.D. projects. Ward recalled the first meeting in Sydney when the costs of the investigation had barely been mentioned — there had been plenty of money to spend then, but no one had thought that results would have been so hard to come by. But perhaps he was prejudging the situation. He turned his back on Pasadena, closing the ranch sliders to the balcony as he returned to the bedroom.

As if in a deep sleep, her blonde hair drawn back from her face, Joanne Varick lay motionless in the hospital bed. Although definite attempts had been made to bring some colour into the private ward it was still clinical in atmosphere and the universal antiseptic odour which fills hospitals from the day they are built, removed any feeling of intimacy or warmth from the room.

Ward sat down on the single chair beside the bed.

'Please wake up, Joanne,' he whispered, knowing she could not hear him.

Christopher Ward had known many women. He had formed brief attachments with some of them whilst others had passed into his life and out again after one or two weeks of mutual enjoyment. One girl who he had met in London shortly after he had joined I.A.S. had wanted Ward to marry her, but her insistence and predisposition towards obvious materialism had eventually driven him away.

In Joanne Varick, Ward had found something that he now realised was what he had been unconsciously searching for. And he had failed her. In a test where Ward's intellectual skills were worthless, he had not been able to protect the girl he loved from what might be permanent disablement.

Yesterday Ward had received a communication from Sydney thanking him for the progress report he had sent. It expressed the view that P.D.3 had not yet produced any worthwhile information and that Ward's theory on the possibly deliberate nature of the accidents was irresponsible speculation on the part of someone who should know better.

Colonel Douglas had strongly advised against any mention of the Ward hypothesis, as they privately called it, and it seemed that his worst fears had been confirmed.

But without the hypothesis, Ward thought, what had P.D.3 really discovered? Viewing his report through the critical eyes of the chiefs of staff of I.A.S. at Sydney, Ward knew that his work must appear unimpressive and rather poor value for money.

So the crashes occurred in fine weather and Ward believed that they were caused by external interference based upon a tenuous theory which had something to do with drugs. The pointed letter had asked rudely if P.D.3 wished to undertake a computer run to check that all aircraft had crashed at night — a fact which had been established many months ago. A lot of money, a lot of words, a stupid theory and no hard facts — the letter was no warning — it was the forerunner of a notification that would cancel the project. Ward knew that barring a breakthrough which would be meaningful to the gentlemen in Sydney, P.D.3 was finished. It was a bitter pill for him to swallow, especially as the results obtained by the other teams were similarly negative if not more so.

Twelve days had elapsed since Ward had returned to work in L.A., and for all of those days and for most of the nights he had driven his staff unmercifully. Passenger information had been refined, cancellation and standby records re-examined and the passage of anti-cyclones across the Pacific plotted in fine detail. Weather maps covered the walls of Ward's office and everywhere the distribution graphs littered the floor filling the spaces between the growing piles of computer print-outs.

The report from Sydney had been prepared and mailed just before the loss of I.A.885, a D.C.8 of Indonesian Airways on its normal route from Darwin in Australia to Suva. Too late, P.D.3 had realised that weather conditions had been suitable; the project was not geared yet for prediction and predictions cannot be made using only one of many hundreds of variables, even though the project co-ordinator was sure that the weather was of profound significance.

Within the next few days, Ward suspected he would be summoned to Australia to be told that P.D.3 would have to be wound up. Or perhaps another letter would be sent — that would be easier for everyone.

He wondered what else I.A.S. or new P.D. teams could hope to accomplish. The situation was out of hand, there was no doubt of that, but what else could be done? Perhaps fighter aircraft would be used to escort passenger planes across the ocean — what a hell of an operation that would be and what would it solve?

One of the ward nurses came into the

room to find Ward sitting gloomily beside the bed his head propped upon his hands.

'It's time, Mr. Ward,' she said.

'If wishing could wake her up she'd be at home in England by now,' Ward answered without moving.

'You're English too, aren't you?'

Ward stood up. 'Yes, I am — I rather wish I hadn't left I'm afraid. If I had stayed there Miss Varick wouldn't be here.' He nodded at the bed.

'She'll get well — I've seen it happen before.'

'That's what everyone tells me but no one knows when. And I'm sure you've seen plenty of deep coma patients who never made it.'

'Some — but never that pretty — now off you go, Mr. Ward, you look as though you could use some sleep — how about an early night.'

Ward grunted, nodding at the two guards on duty outside the door as he left the ward.

He felt drained of all energy and frustrated.

Glen Yesler was waiting for him at the

front entrance of the Military Hospital.

'No change,' Ward said, 'I'm tired of saying those two words — I don't think she's going to come out of it.'

Yesler was silent as they walked to the car. He spoke just as they reached the Pontiac. 'The Colonel told me about the project,' he said gruffly.

Ward looked at him across the shiny black roof of the car.

'If I could have five more minutes with the bastards who did that to Miss Varick, maybe I'd feel a little better,' he said, 'my bare hands would do — no chain saw this time.'

Yesler shook his head. 'It doesn't work. I saw two Vietnamese once — a father and grandfather — they caught up with a couple of guys who set fire to a house with the rest of the family in it.'

'Go on,' Ward said.

'We didn't stop them — I was a bit younger then and a lot more stupid.' Yesler smiled briefly. 'They killed them slowly — I still get dreams.'

'And afterwards?'

'That's just it, Mr. Ward — afterwards

nothing.' Yesler spread his hands palm upwards on the roof. 'It didn't ease their pain — maybe even made it worse or last longer.'

'You mean revenge is not sweet?'

'That's how I figure it.'

Ward climbed into the passenger seat. 'Let's go, Glen,' he said shortly.

It was some miles later when he spoke again.

'Do you think the authorities will ever discover why Miss Varick and I were attacked at the cabin — I mean who organised it?'

'You know as much as I do, Mr. Ward — one of them mentioned P.D.3 so they must have known a little, but almost certainly they were just given some dough and told what to do — my country has too many killers of that kind. They weren't bright enough to know what P.D.3 is doing and they haven't given any lead on who paid them.'

'Perhaps the questions weren't put forcibly enough,' Ward said with malice.

Yesler gave a quick smile. 'Don't worry about that,' he said, 'I've seen those guys in Military Intelligence at work. I get dreams about that too.'

'So what do I do, Glen — suppose the project is cancelled,' Ward was finding it easy to talk to this previously somewhat inhibited young man. It was a refreshing change from the endless discussions with Ralph Douglas and the others at the project.

Yesler shrugged. 'It depends on how right you reckon you are — Colonel Douglas told me you had a hunch — that's all he told me,' he added hurriedly. 'If you feel real strongly, then I figure you should keep at it — but I don't know, Mr. Ward — you have to sort it out yourself, don't you.'

'I can't keep at it as you say — not without a project,' Ward said.

'Okay, so you're beat; quit and go home.'

Ward stared at the neon signs streaming past the windows of the car. Quit? Give up and return to England? Perhaps it wouldn't come to that — P.D.3 wasn't dead yet.

But when Christopher Ward arrived at

his office on the following morning and saw the two big manila envelopes on his desk, he knew that his project was over.

When Mary Cawston brought his coffee the envelopes were still unopened.

'They were delivered by hand,' she said, 'a helicopter from the terminal brought the first one. The other one came by car — from the terminal too.'

'One from Sydney and one from I.A.S. in London,' Ward said, 'both saying the same thing — I don't need to open them.'

His secretary reached for the letter opener and slit the official seals. She shook out the sheets of expensive white paper onto the desk top.

Ward's expression remained unchanged as he read the polite directions contained in the two formal communications.

'My job in London is still open,' he said bitterly, 'isn't that nice of them?'

'How long do we have to run down?' Mary Cawston asked.

'Two days from now P.D.3 ceases to exist, all staff will be paid off — three months salary to help them get over the sour taste in their mouths — some of us will be assigned to other areas.'

Ward threw the pieces of paper into his waste bin. 'The shortsighted fools,' he said calmly, 'I hope they never find an answer.'

'You don't mean that, chief.'

He paused before answering. 'No, I don't — someone has to find out. I'm just upset, Mary, everything seems to have gone wrong and I'm not used to failure. I suppose I must have been too confident — I still am — isn't that funny.'

'Maybe you didn't word that report in the right way. You were a bit blunt at the beginning and remember Colonel Douglas thought we shouldn't have put in the Ward hypothesis. The Colonel knows how the chiefs of staff think.'

'Anyway, it doesn't matter now,' Ward said, 'I suppose I'll have to call a meeting straight away — I'll speak to divisional heads in here — organise it for ten o'clock sharp, please.'

When she had left the room Ward picked up his telephone to call Douglas.

'I suppose you already know?' Ward said.

'Yes, I got my own letter — hell I'm sorry Chris.'

'I've scheduled a meeting for ten o'clock, the sooner everyone knows the better.'

'What are you going to do?' Douglas asked.

'One of your guys summed up the situation when I was talking to him last night; he said I was beaten and that without a project I had no alternative but to quit.'

'You'll resign?'

'I don't know, Ralph — London said I could have my old job back there.'

'Joanne wouldn't want you to quit.'

'Leave her out of this,' Ward snapped. 'I'll see you at ten.'

He leant back in the swivel chair and tried to think.

Old Doctor Bateman would be laughing, Ward thought wryly, remembering his early criticism of the statistical approach. Perhaps he had been correct in his assessment of the chances of success — P.D.3 had taken too long.

Ward picked up the blue telephone

from his desk, toying with the idea of calling Australia to find out whether the other projects had suffered a similar fate. A chat with Frank Macklin, who was still in Sydney, could clear the air but what could be gained? There was no chance of reopening P.D.3 and no comfort would be drawn from the knowledge that other project groups had been instructed to disband. He replaced the receiver, pushed a nagging desire to think about Joanne to the back of his mind and began to prepare notes for his final discourse.

Opening the meeting, Ward kept it short and sweet allowing no emotion to show in his face as he passed on the blunt instructions from headquarters.

Grouped in the office, the men who had worked with the tall bearded Englishman knew how much it must have cost him to make the announcement. Aware that P.D.3 had not discovered the degree of correlation between the crashes which had been anticipated, they nevertheless had full confidence in Ward and in the project. It was only a matter of time — no one on the staff doubted that simple fact — but now Ward had suffered a personal blow to his ego and there was no more time left.

Respect for the co-ordinator of the project had been high from the day that P.D.3 had been formed, many of the departmental heads having worked with Ward before. His valiant attempt to save himself and Joanne Varick during the raid at the cabin had been widely discussed amongst the staff, despite the fact that the entire incident was not supposed to have been disclosed to anyone. Christopher Ward was in the company of friends, not colleagues or employees.

Because of their respect, eyes were lowered awkwardly to the floor and there were no questions. Knowing there was nothing to be said when Ward had concluded, people shuffled out of the door returning to their own offices or pausing in the corridor to discuss the news.

Three men remained in Ward's office. Douglas stood hands in pockets staring through the venetian blinds at the smog outside. Steven Berros, head or ex head of passenger records, wanted to say something to Ward.

'I'll be going back to Convair tomorrow,' he said, 'I'd sure like to see you take that appointment as chief of computer modelling in the Weapon System Division.'

'I don't know what I'm going to do yet, Steve,' Ward said, 'I'll see you before you go though.' He held out his hand. 'And thanks,' he said, 'thanks for everything.'

The third man in the room had remained seated until now. Graham Redlands, a thickset individual in his early fifties with an unruly mop of pure white hair, was not given to speak frequently. As head of the meteorological data department he had worked furiously to produce all of the information that was necessary for the computer analyses and was regarded internationally as an expert on weather prediction methods.

'Have you got a job for me too?' Ward smiled at him.

Redland's grizzled countenance returned the smile. 'Who'd employ a cocky young punk like you,' he replied in his usual growl. 'Anyway, I don't think you're finished with the job yet.'

From his briefcase he withdrew a folded sheet of thick white paper which he placed on Ward's desk.

'Now then,' he said, 'seeing as how P.D.3 is closed down, or will be in a couple of days, you may not be interested in what I have here. On the other hand, you might be interested but think I'm off my head.'

'What have you got this time, Graham?' Ralph Douglas asked. He had ceased staring out the window and had joined Ward behind his desk.

'A weather map — another weather map — what else?'

Ward unfolded it, placing a paper weight and a slide rule at the ends of the sheet in order to hold it flat.

The map appeared familiar. Covering a large area of the Pacific between the equator and the tropic of Capricorn, its left hand margin sliced through Indonesia whilst the right hand extremity terminated at a point some hundreds of miles east of the Tongan Islands.

Centred just to the left of a point midway between the New Hebrides and the islands of the Fijian group, an impressive anticyclone dominated the weather situation. Several notes in Redlands's neat writing followed the isobars across the paper.

After several minutes' study, during which he read some of the pencilled notes, Ward straightened.

'When did you draw this one?' he asked.

'Last night — I had to guess a little but this morning's data confirms it almost exactly.'

'So this is the position right now — is that what you mean?' Douglas asked.

Redlands inspected his watch. 'In a couple of hours that's how it'll look.' He smiled again. 'I don't need to remind you of the met man's escape clause do I?'

'And the pressure and cloud?' Ward said.

'A good solid high, some cirrus — streaky ones and no sign of them thickening into cirrostratus. It's even a better picture than the one three days ago, if you can believe such a thing.'

Colonel Douglas lit a cigarette. 'Have you got the I.A.885 map handy, Graham?'

From his briefcase Redlands produced a thin transparent sheet of plastic, aligning it over the map by means of three reference dots.

'I think I'm ahead of you,' he said.

The plastic film also had an anticyclone drawn upon it. This time the centre of the high pressure area was situated well to the west of Espiritu Santo, the largest island in the New Hebrides.

Ward nodded to no one in particular. 'So you were wrong,' he said, 'it carried on moving as it's supposed to, west to east and if anything it's more stable than ever — very settled indeed.'

'Yeah, I was wrong about what would happen to it after I.A.885 — I could be wrong this time too.'

Unwilling to be the first to broach the subject, each of the three men continued to focus their attention on the map.

Ward broke the thoughtful silence suddenly. 'And I suppose the satellite high altitude photos confirm this?'

'They do,' Redlands said, 'do you want to see them, I have them here?'

'No,' Ward shook his head, 'what about met information from any surface vessels or aircraft still flying around there?'

'I wouldn't be here now if everything hadn't pointed to it, Chris.'

'Okay, Graham,' Douglas said, 'another super exceptional patch of calm weather has formed, or rather reformed, over the Pacific in our investigation zone — so what?'

'You're the clever guys, not me,' Redlands said disarmingly, 'I'm only a simple met man.'

'Cut it out,' Ward said sharply, almost wishing that this unexpected turn in events had not taken place.

He placed both palms on the map and looked at Redlands for several seconds before he spoke.

'You think this is going to be number six, don't you?'

'I don't need two digital computers to help me think.' Redlands answered, 'any guy here in my department could pick this one; yes, Chris, this could be number six, but I hope like hell I'm wrong.'

'There seems to be a damned lot of good weather about in the Pacific lately,' Douglas said, 'I thought only three days a year were as calm as this.'

'Statistics are statistics,' Redlands replied easily, 'and weather is weather — take your choice.'

'Goddam!' Ward shouted, thumping his fist on the desk, 'we can't predict another crash just because the weather happens to be right. We're supposed to be trained men; you can't correlate with one single lousy variable. Nobody would believe us and we shouldn't be so bloody stupid. Our minds are addled — crystal ball men, that's what we've become — no wonder they axed P.D.3.'

'That's fine then,' the Colonel said, 'we'll all forget about it and then when there's another disaster — another hundred dead people — we can say that we were right all along.' He stubbed out his cigarette with unnecessary force.

Redlands and Douglas were both looking at Ward.

'What the hell do you want me to say?' he said. 'I have no authority now — only to wind up the project. I have no support staff and no equipment. And I'm not going to make a bloody fool of myself over this,' he hammered the weather map again.

Quietly Redlands spoke. 'Okay, Chris, you're unemployed — busted and angry. Maybe that's good. It seems to me that here is the opportunity for us to get off our backsides once and for all. Go grab a plane and get the hell out there where it's going to happen, it's the only way we're ever going to find out.'

'What?'

Redlands refused to answer, his blue eyes boring into Ward.

'I can't allow that,' Douglas intervened. 'You can't stop him either, Colonel,' Redlands said. 'What's Chris got to lose?'

'His life, maybe,' Douglas answered shortly, 'what the hell could he find out anyway?'

'For God's sake shut up both of you,' Ward said angrily.

'I haven't said I'm going anywhere.

Now will you please leave me alone, I am still project co-ordinator around here and I want time to think.'

'I'll leave the maps,' Redlands said, 'you know where to find me don't you.'

The Colonel placed a hand on Ward's shoulder as he started to say something but the younger man shrugged it off and deliberately turned his back.

Soon Christopher Ward was alone in his office, his brain racing furiously as he paced from one wall to another seeking an answer to an unanswerable problem.

If he had been older, or perhaps if Joanne Varick had not lain unconscious in hospital, he would have decided differently. Later he was to regret the outcome of his deliberations on this afternoon, but Ward was hurt, angry, frustrated and concerned. Under the circumstances it was not surprising that he reached the judgement that he did.

At nine o'clock that evening, with P.D.3 firmly behind him, Christopher Ward boarded a long distance flight from Los Angeles bound for Hawaii and Fiji.

7

It was with very mixed feelings that Ward embarked upon his single-handed venture to discover the cause of the air tragedies. For the first time in his life he was to work alone, there were no highly trained specialists to back him up and no protective umbrella of a large organisation to shelter beneath if things went wrong on this occasion.

Ward was aware of the sense of challenge in his isolation, stimulated even by the rash decision he had made. To be able to work completely alone was refreshing after the many years of project team work.

Adding to what he recognised as an overall sensation of excitement, was the experience of relief at shedding the not inconsiderable responsibility of P.D.3.

Only two people knew where Ward was bound for, Colonel Ralph Douglas and Graham Redlands, both of them sworn to secrecy — not only to safeguard Ward — but to protect themselves from obvious criticism should the enterprise ever become known. And, because Ward had felt that he was running out on the girl he loved, an envelope had been lodged in trust for Joanne Varick which would be delivered to her as soon as she regained consciousness.

With only these slender ties with the world with which he was familiar, Ward had launched himself upon a one man crusade. His wits and his intellect would have to be used to keep him from now on and suddenly he realised how ill equipped he actually was. It was too easy to remember the weekend at Devil's Canyon where intelligence and logic had not been enough — animal cunning and plain physical ability being more useful in circumstances of that kind.

It had taken Redlands the best part of an hour to talk a reluctant Douglas into backing the undertaking, the tough old met man finally persuading the incorruptible Colonel to offer certain unique services that Military Intelligence were well able to provide.

By the time Ward had left the El Segundo building his beard had been reshaped, his clothes replaced and his name changed. He owned a new passport — an American one — and carried a slim air travel case with a double-skinned lid.

Hardly knowing himself, torn with uncertainty and disbelieving that it was really happening, Justin Nielhart from Boston — alias Christopher Ward of London — had climbed aboard the 707 with the other passengers noting that his hand baggage was deliberately passed high above the metal detector and not through it. Douglas had explained that M.I. would extend their influence as far as Hawaii, the first stop for the aircraft — thereafter it had been agreed that it would be better for Ward to rely on his own initiative.

There had been no good-byes and Ward had driven himself the short distance to the air terminal, almost needing the accustomed companionship of Glen Yesler. He already felt slightly lonely although the excitement still

123

tended to override all other emotions; the whole thing had taken place so damned quickly he thought.

As a final demonstration of efficiency, the Colonel had arranged for the other two seats in Ward's row to be unoccupied providing welcome space for Ward's long legs. Knowing that other passengers could board at Honolulu, removing the advantage of additional room beside him, Ward opened his travel case and extracted the drawing which Redlands had produced just before he had left P.D.3 for the last time.

Spreading it open upon the table in front of him, he studied the familiar pattern of the islands dotted across the sheet of paper. Redlands had shifted the centre of the high pressure area slightly more to the east in order to bring the map even further up to date. In fact the anticyclone was so large that the fine weather would extend over many thousands of square miles and the exact position of its centre was of little importance.

More interesting than the isobars and

the pencilled notes that always smothered the weather maps which Graham Redlands drew, were the fine red lines that traversed the open centre of the high pressure zone. Under ordinary circumstances there would have been a network of these lines for these were the flight paths of all scheduled passenger aircraft that would pass through the exceptionally fine weather during the next three days. Since the loss of I.A.885, virtually all of the airlines with business in the South Pacific had suspended their flights at least temporarily and there were only three aircraft officially listed as flying anywhere near the New Hebrides or the Fijian islands in the immediate future. One of them was in the air at the moment and Christopher Ward was on it.

It would be ironic, he thought, if this 707 was to be the one that would suffer the sixth mishap. Statistically, and Ward naturally found it difficult to avoid such an approach, there was a thirty three and a third per cent chance that he was on board a fated plane. The possibility that he would be a passenger on number six had not been overlooked by the three men who had planned this venture.

Although many theories had been put forward in an attempt to explain how a modern jet could be brought down without the crew having sufficient time to radio vital information, none seemed so likely as instant decompression. A bomb inside the fuselage that would be capable of blasting a fair sized hole would do the job quite well, but even then, providing the crew had survived, there would still be time to transmit the position of the plane and even perhaps explain what had happened. Under current regulations concerning the inspection of luggage for metallic objects, it was unlikely in the extreme that a bomb could be loaded on board and Ward knew the idea was somewhat unrealistic.

Nevertheless, he had received detailed survival instructions and clipped inside Ward's case was a small personal oxygen breathing set similar in configuration to the dangerous equipment used by some underwater divers in shallow water. For a short while, indeed, the unit could be

126

used for breathing under water, but Ward very much hoped that he would have no need of the device either in the air or beneath the sea.

Also in Ward's case lay a thin plastic life jacket which would inflate automatically on contact with the water, a miniature but powerful radio transmitter having batteries that were activated by sea water and a Model 39 Smith and Wesson nine millimetre double action automatic. Christopher Ward was equipped as well as any foreign agent, but was acutely conscious of the unhappy fact that he himself was hopelessly out of his depth in the field of espionage, crime and mass murder.

Pushing thoughts of survival and violence to one side — there would be time enough to become frightened later — he leant back in his seat deciding that the four plain clothes security men who travelled on every 707 would be better able to handle danger from within. On the other hand, each of the planes that had crashed had carried their full complement of security guards, men that had died with the rest of the passengers.

Then, to add to Ward's discomfort, he suddenly realised that Redlands had forgotten something. He grabbed the map to confirm his suspicions.

Not thirty three and a third percent — fifty! One of the aircraft would pass through the anticyclone in daylight. Everyone inside and outside P.D.3 knew that the disasters happened exclusively during the hours of darkness.

If Ward reached Nandi safely — and now there was only an even chance that he would if his theory was right — there would only be one other flight that would pass through the danger area. Redlands had predicted that in three days time the weather would break — the accuracy of the prediction Ward did not doubt for a moment — Redlands had a rare gift for making such prophecies. Thus Ward was already on one of the risky flights and in another two days he would somehow have to be in a position to observe the other one.

It was with remarkable slowness that the full impact of this latest discovery entered Ward's rapier like brain. The logic was inescapable. If Ward reached Fiji, then only one other possibility remained. To fly on the other aircraft would be suicide if the three senior men of P.D.3 had guessed correctly — a one hundred per cent chance of dying!

Ward studied the route that the second plane would follow, wondering if he should attempt to prevent the flight from taking place — always assuming he was still in a position to attempt anything, he thought uneasily. A more interesting notion hovered at the corner of his mind; if he vanished with this aircraft the chances were that the other flight would be quite safe, no two planes had ever disappeared within a few days of each other. It was a game of logic and he was not at all sure that he had acted wisely in deciding to play.

The hostess was asking Ward to remove his map from the table so that she could serve his dinner. Mechanically he refolded the paper, wondering again if he had been stupid in embarking upon this foolhardy adventure. He was still bandaged about his abdomen and still suffered pain if he attempted to bend forwards or twist his body sideways. He had no definite plan of campaign and very little time in which to originate one — perhaps Douglas had been right — a fit and trained young man from Military Intelligence would have been a more suitable choice.

While he ate, Ward persuaded himself that the thin correlation that had been responsible for this flight to Fiji could easily be wrong; the whole thing was a literal flight of fancy and he was tired of the endless thinking. The meal was unpalatable to him in his current frame of mind.

He pressed the tip of the arm rest to recline his seat and drifted into a confused sleep.

Much later that night, Christopher Ward as Justin Nielhart officially left the United States of America at the emigration counter of the Honolulu air terminal. From this point onwards he would be quite alone, outside the jurisdiction of the American authorities and without the protection of the defunct P.D.3 organisation. His previous association with I.A.S. could easily be used in an emergency but Ward knew that it was essential for him to remain anonymous for as long as possible. If the crashes had been deliberately engineered as he suspected, it was better for him to be Justin Nielhart; the pretence would not have to be maintained for very long.

The flight from Honolulu to Nandi was the worst that Ward had ever had the misfortune to make. Very tired now, with his ribs hurting from the hours of enforced idleness and because his body had remained too long in one position, he tried to keep alert, concentrating on every move in the passenger cabin and listening to every tiny variation in the suppressed roar from the four engines.

Most occupants of the economy class section had extinguished their reading lights, the atmosphere being one of bored relaxation throughout the plane. An occasional weak bladdered passenger wandered past the tense Englishman to the toilets only to wander back again a few minutes later, whilst a young couple on their honeymoon, sitting four rows in front of Ward, refused to believe that anyone else was awake. Their enthusiastic and frequently indecent wrestling caused Ward to start from his seat on several occasions thinking that whatever it was that was going to happen had finally begun. But the 707 flew on uninterrupted through the warm night, crossing the international dateline and steadily crawling along the red stripe on Ward's map.

At four thirty five local time, six hundred miles out from Nandi, Ward estimated that this flight had half an hour to live if it had been earmarked for tragedy. He tightened his seat belt until it hurt and waited; and waited.

Three quarters of an hour later, after breakfast, the passengers readied themselves for landing. In a seat near the centre of the cabin, a washed out, relieved and still nervous Justin Nielhart released the tension from his seat belt and removed the case that had been supported on his knees for the last five hundred miles. Phase one of the operation was over. More certainty would be

132

attached to phase two and Ward had decided upon one vital difference that would be made in approach next time. He would not be on board the second plane.

Traces of dawn were streaking the dark night clouds which had gathered over Viti Levu, the main island of the Fijian group. As the plane descended, penetrating thin layers of fine mist, Ward caught a glimpse of the sombre coast; the tropical vegetation, sparkling blue sea and sandy beaches appearing only as shades of black so early in the morning. Very soon, the sun would transform the scene into the south sea paradise of the travel brochures, but even now, as the captain lined up for his final approach, there was a sense of mystery emanating from the island and the surrounding ocean.

Ward had visited Fiji only twice before, the last time during his return flight from Sydney to L.A. On both occasions some of the fascination of the islands that affects some people had rubbed off on him and he was pleased to be here again. Whether or not he would have time to see something of the country on this trip remained to be seen; he had but one day in which to decide upon a plan and what would happen after that he could only guess at.

By the time the plane had come to rest near the tiny terminal building Ward had recovered his composure, although the inevitable fatigue that follows a moderately long flight had not yet dispersed and his rib cage felt a little sore. He checked that the secret compartment in the lid of his case containing the radio and his gun was securely fastened before joining the queue of other passengers waiting impatiently to disembark.

Outside the plane the heat was oppressive even though the day was so young. Perspiration had thoroughly soaked Ward's bandage well before he reached the customs counter making him long to shed the suit he wore.

Nervously he flipped open the catches on his case, sliding it across the counter. Dressed more comfortably than Ward in traditional native costume, the pleasant faced Fijian official frowned at the oxygen equipment. 'Scuba gear is pretty cheap here,' he said, 'I didn't think anyone used these any more.'

'I've had it for years,' Ward answered easily, 'but I've only used it a couple of times — I know all about excessive oxygen in my blood — maybe I'll pick up a decent set of bottles here; I don't know yet.'

The officer chalked an indecipherable mark on the case and wished Ward an enjoyable stay.

Relieved, but becoming hotter by the minute, Ward walked through the door into the arrival lounge where he headed for the bar.

He had barely finished placing his order when the unfamiliar but easily recognisable name of Nielhart came over the public address speakers. Waiting for the message to be repeated whilst gulping his iced drink and pocketing the change, he wondered what had caused Douglas or Redlands to dispatch a communication ahead of his flight.

He collected a slip of paper from the information desk and leant against the wall to read it.

'Flight T.E.389 will take place in daylight. Suggest you concentrate on M.P.173 only. Good luck.'

Ward crumpled the message and thrust it in his pocket; what a waste of time he thought, as if they believed he was too stupid to have worked it out for himself.

M.P.173 was the only flight left now that he had arrived safely in Viti Levu and Ward had thirty six hours in which to act. The D.C. super 8 of Malaysian Pacific would be in the air in the right place in what really was a very short time — Ward was going to have to move quickly.

There was work to be done here in the terminal first.

He retired to the gentlemen's washroom where he showered after removing the already sodden length of bandage; from now on Ward's ribs would have to hold themselves together. After shaving he changed into a white short sleeved shirt and a pair of smart shorts, replacing his shoes with a pair of thongs which he had brought from the States.

More suitably dressed and very much

more comfortable Ward felt ready to undertake the first part of the vague plan that he had finally decided to follow.

Returning to the information desk, he addressed the pretty girl with the flower in her hair.

'My name's Nielhart,' Ward introduced himself. 'I wonder if you could tell me if it's possible to charter a light plane from here?'

'I'm afraid I'm not sure, sir. I know Air Polynesia operate small planes but I think they're all on scheduled flights, not on charter. If you care to wait for a moment I can make some enquiries for you.'

She picked up her telephone and dialled a number.

After a brief conversation she replaced the receiver.

'There are only two airlines,' she said to Ward, 'one's called Coral Coast Airlines and operates from here — you can get details from the Air Polynesia counter down there,' she pointed towards the departure lounge.

'And the other?' Ward enquired.

'It's just one plane — it flies from Malolo Lailai.'

'How do I find out about it?'

'You'll probably have to go over to the island and ask. I'm afraid I can't help you very much, Mr. Nielhart.'

Ward thanked her and made his way to the counter where the red Air Polynesian insignia was displayed.

A young European with a pronounced French accent answered Ward's queries.

'Ah Monsieur — we have one French Jodel — a very small plane, no? — two Piper P.A.18's and one Italian Procaer Picchio.'

Ward was familiar only with the Piper. 'And the Pipers are available for charter?' he said.

'None are available,' the young man spread open his arms; 'the rich Americans you understand — all are booked for at least the next four days.'

'I can afford to pay a great deal,' Ward said, a feeling of despair creeping over him.

'Coral Coast Airlines are not able to help you, Monsieur — I am sorry.'

138

A day ago, Ward would have had sufficient authority to demand that an aircraft be made available for his use — now, when he needed authority more than ever before, he was powerless.

Realising that it was probably pointless to argue with the man behind the counter, Ward turned on his heel and walked to the exit.

Outside, there was a fragrance in the morning air and the humidity had risen making the atmosphere feel rather like that of a heated glass-house.

Ward approached a waiting taxi. 'I have to get to Malolo Lailai in a hurry,' he said through the open window, 'I know it's another island and that's all.'

Accustomed to dealing with such ignorance from long experience with the droves of tourists that visit the island in the cooler months, the driver proceeded to open the door of the car.

'I drive you to Lautoka,' he said, 'then you may take the hydrofoil. If you were not in a hurry I would advise the cruise on the schooner, but that will take nearly two and a half hours.'

'I understand there's a plane available for charter there,' Ward said. 'I don't suppose you know where I should go or who to see?'

The car had reached Lautoka before the driver had finished warning his passenger about the mad American with the old amphibian who lived on the tiny offshore island.

'He is what we call an island bum,' he said to Ward as he searched for the change for the fare, 'he lives off the tourists and spends all of his money on whisky; you should not fly in his plane, it is too dangerous.'

Knowing that he would be fortunate if he were able to hire a plane at all, the cautionary advice did not disturb Ward unduly. He boarded the hydrofoil optimistically, hoping that the trip to Malolo Lailai was not going to be a waste of valuable time.

But Ward was in luck. Trudging along the beach of Plantation village, a vacation settlement of delightful thatched bures that nestled amongst the tall palms, he could see the amphibian parked upon a

140

concrete ramp. Further up the beach a corrugated iron hut displayed a badly written sign advertising flights.

Hoping that the owner of the business would be on hand, Ward reduced his pace, walking down onto the harder sand and letting the small waves break over his feet.

To his right, the miniature village appeared almost unreal so artificially beautiful was it in the clear sunshine. A few people mingled with the backdrop of palm trees and here and there a sulu clad Fijian girl would wander from one of the many bures. An island paradise, Ward thought — it really was as he had pictured it — a dramatic contrast with Los Angeles and the city of his home in England. One day he would bring Joanne here, if —

The aircraft was a Grumman Widgeon — an old one and a battered one. It was a faded pale blue where the paint was not peeling off. To prevent the plane from rolling down the ramp into the water, two half-round fence posts had been used as chocks behind the wheels and on either side of the concrete slope the beautiful white sand was littered with bottles.

Ward approached the office but found it deserted. Wondering what to do next, his attention was attracted by a hearty yell from the palm trees where a figure in a dirty white shirt was running towards him.

Hoping that this would be the pilot Ward walked to meet him.

Somewhat out of breath from his sprint, the man stopped and stuck out his hand. 'I'm Jack Fielding,' he announced, 'are you looking for me?'

He was younger than Ward had expected from the description that the taxi driver had given him. Sandy coloured hair of considerable length surrounded an open face burnt dark brown by the sun. Fielding wore no shoes, a pair of faded denim shorts and an oil stained shirt with no buttons. Without asking, Ward knew he had found the man he was looking for.

Ward introduced himself as Justin Nielhart. 'I believe you run a charter service,' he said.

'Run anything you want,' Fielding

replied smiling. 'Where do you want to go — or do you just want a round the islands sight-see?'

'I want to do something rather odd,' Ward said. 'Is there somewhere we can talk?'

'Ah — come to the office — we will conduct our business there.' Fielding led the way down the beach to the corrugated iron hut. He disappeared inside for a moment and came out clutching a pencil and paper and a large unopened bottle of Coca Cola.

'Sit down, Mr. Nielhart.' Fielding generously offered his prospective customer a piece of beach. 'And tell me about your odd request.'

Ward opened his case and removed an unmarked map covering the same area as the one that Redlands had drawn. Across it Ward had pencilled the straight route of Malaysian Pacific flight 173.

'You see this line?' he said, 'I want you to fly me from here to the nearest point on it which would be about there,' Ward drew a small cross. 'From there we travel as far as we can along the line towards the

143

New Hebrides — all the way if you can carry enough fuel.'

Fielding stared at the map. 'What the hell for?' he asked curiously.

'For money and no questions.'

'When?'

'Starting tomorrow at the latest.'

'Mr. Nielhart, I'm your man. Now let's find out if you mean business — this little trip is going to cost you quite a packet.' He opened the bottle with a pen knife and started drinking. 'Trying to kick the hard stuff,' he explained. 'How much will you offer?'

8

Christopher Ward, one-time senior executive of the vast International Air Security Organisation, had become enraptured with the idyllic island paradise of Malolo Lailai. A mere twenty four hours on the golden sand had transformed him.

Since his arrival at the beach where Fielding kept his elderly amphibian he had not left the edge of the copra plantation, spending his time in evading the questions of the American pilot and in soaking up the glorious sunshine. As Redlands had promised, the weather was quite perfect although rather hot, the soft tradewinds being unusually absent from the beach.

By early evening Ward had the importance of his mission firmly in perspective, Fielding's charmingly irresponsible outlook on life proving to be extremely contagious.

The owner of the Widgeon had refused

to leave Ward to his own devices and had spent all day talking about himself and about life in the islands. He had also generously insisted on Ward sleeping the night in the bure that Fielding apparently either owned or rented from the local plantation manager.

Ward had been treated to a verbal tour of Melanesia, Fielding seeming as though he knew each and every one of the three hundred and twenty tiny islands. The pilot had spent the past six years in Fiji, making just enough money from his one man airline to enable him to live as he pleased. Fielding could describe dense forests on the windward slopes of Taveuni and Kandavu as though he had been born there. At his fingertips were the export quantities of copra, banana, coconut, sugar cane, taro and all of the other produce of the islands, whilst his knowledge of the sea and the creatures in it was so extensive that Ward thought that the pilot must at one time have made a deep study of the subject. As is so very often the case, Fielding's way of life belied the sensitivity of the man and during the day Ward had progressively warmed to the friendly American.

Fielding had two problems, drink and a mild weakness for the native girls. Three or four times a year he embarked upon a cure for the former; he was in the middle of one of these at the moment. The attraction that the local girls seemed to have for the easy living pilot was not encouraged but neither was it denied and as Fielding did not regard his weakness as such, he did nothing to change his licentious habits.

The years had drifted by for Jack Fielding; he was content, a condition that half the civilised world was unable to achieve. Ward envied him and found his company most engaging. The day had passed quickly and pleasantly into evening when Ward retired early to bed more tired than even he had realised.

Fielding's house girl had woken Ward half an hour ago just in time for him to witness the spectacular Fijian sunrise. He had finished eating a simple breakfast and was about to start looking for Fielding when the pilot appeared.

'Well, hi,' Fielding greeted Ward.

'Good morning — are you ready?'

'Yeah, the old bird's got all the gas I can squeeze into her tanks and I've given her the usual pre-flight check,' Fielding grinned.

The two men walked together down the beach. When they reached the plane the pilot turned. 'I still want to know why the hell you want to fly along that line on your map,' he said, giving Ward the impression that he might change his mind unless he received an answer this time.

'I've already told you — I'm looking for something,' Ward said.

'What?'

'I don't know.'

The American shook his head as if amazed. 'And if we don't find this thing that you don't know what you're looking for, it's cost you a hundred dollars an hour for nothing?'

'That's right,' Ward answered easily.

'You must know — I mean you must have some idea what you're expecting to find — do we look up or down or at each other?'

'No, really,' Ward said amused at Fielding's expression of disbelief, 'I haven't the slightest idea what I'm expecting to see; we probably won't find anything.'

'Well in that case, Mr. Nielhart, we had better start right away — it sounds to me as if we are going to have to do a hell of a lot of looking.'

The Widgeon was in much better condition than its external appearance would indicate. Built by the Grumman Aircraft Corporation in 1946, the original twin Ranger engines had been replaced by a pair of two hundred and sixty horsepower fuel injected Continentals, giving the plane a cruising speed of a hundred and forty miles an hour and the airframe was sound and particularly well maintained.

Fielding had already let the amphibian roll down the ramp into the calm water and the two men had to wade out to it from the beach in order to climb aboard.

'It's one of the tremendous advantages of these things,' Fielding said, 'they can take off in very shallow water and skim across a coral reef without tearing their guts out. The wheels are good too — I'd hate to have a float plane that I couldn't drive up on the beach — I've had this one tied to palm trees before now when a hurricane's got going.'

The Widgeon boasted four seats in the main cabin and two in the cockpit. Fielding indicated that Ward should sit beside him at the front.

Both engines started without effort, the exhausts spitting blue smoke for a moment before all cylinders were firing evenly. The American eased the throttles open a little to warm up the engines causing the plane to move sluggishly away from the beach. After a few minutes he nodded to Ward and pulled back on the controls.

Leaving a pure white wake in a glittering stream from the edge of the sand, the Widgeon accelerated until the fuselage began to plane. Seconds later the transformation from boat to aircraft took place and Ward was on yet another leg of his quest.

From the air the islands appeared a

very dark green, seeming almost to be floating on the unnaturally placid ocean. A few small fishing boats dotted the blue Pacific, some of them leaving short white tails behind as they moved away from the coastline. It was an exceptionally beautiful sight.

Once Fielding had reached two thousand feet, he reduced the rate of climb and adjusted his course to intersect with the line on Ward's map.

'You remember what I said about fuel,' he said.

'Four hours maximum you mean?' Ward answered.

'Yeah — at a hundred and forty miles per hour we can manage a total range of five hundred and sixty miles — say two hundred and fifty out before we turn back.'

Ward inspected the coloured map fixed to the wall of the cockpit.

'Couldn't we make Noumea in New Caledonia or Port Vila in the New Hebrides?' he asked.

Fielding looked pained. 'I operate out of Fiji, Mr. Nielhart — I have what you

151

might call poor international relations outside of there.'

Ward did not press the point, but still doubted that a two hundred and fifty mile sweep along the flight path of M.P.173 would be far enough.

The D.C. super 8 would start its journey from Singapore calling at Djakarta and at Darwin in Australia before commencing the long Pacific flight to Mexico City. During the coming night the aircraft would fly through the danger zone and, before it did so, Christopher Ward wanted to have satisfied himself that the corridor was obviously clear. It was a foolish idea he realised gazing around him. Open cloudless sky and endless blue sea — what could he hope to discover? A fast fighter plane, an internal bomb or sabotage — that's what he should be looking for and none of these would ever be found by cruising about in the Widgeon.

Fielding was looking at him curiously. 'That line,' he said, 'it's a flight route isn't it?'

Ward nodded slowly.

'And there are not many scheduled flights still operating around here are there?'

'No.'

'But this one's special to you?'

Ward remained silent.

'The crashes,' Fielding said quietly, 'it's something to do with all those disappearing planes; you're here to try and find out aren't you, Mr. Nielhart?'

There was no reason to deny what must now seem an obvious reason for his presence in Fielding's Widgeon.

'That's right,' Ward said, 'but it's supposed to be a secret.'

Fielding was looking thoughtful, the corners of his eyes and his forehead crinkling with the frown on his tanned face.

'But you really don't know what you're looking for?'

Ward explained, simplifying the position and omitting all reference to P.D.3 or the work that had been carried out in Los Angeles.

When he had finished Fielding made a brief announcement.

'You're mad,' he said, 'completely bloody mad — there's nothing out here but sea and sky, millions of square miles of it.'

'I still have to look,' Ward said, almost apologetically, 'it's all there is left to do.'

'But what about all the other flights?'

'Just this one, Fielding.'

'You already know that this one — ?' Fielding didn't finish the sentence.

'Only think or believe, but I've got to look.'

No more was said for the next sixty minutes, Fielding concentrating on following his allotted course whilst absorbing the information Ward had given him. Ward himself gradually became hypnotised by the vastness of the environment surrounding the diminutive amphibian as far as his eyes could see.

One hundred and eighty miles out from Viti Levu the monotony was broken. Ten thousand feet below, appearing motionless on the glass-like sea, a black coaster could be seen through the forward window of the cockpit.

'There you are,' Fielding said sarcastically, 'besides the sea and the sky that's all we've seen so far and I bet you fifty bucks that's all we're going to see.'

Ward stared at the ship trying to make his brain function. Soon the Widgeon had left the lonely vessel behind as the amphibian flew onwards heading for the minuscule Santa Cruz islands.

A half an hour later, seventy miles further on, Fielding banked his plane.

'Two fifty,' he said, 'that's half way, Mr. Nielhart — we have to go back.'

Ward consulted the weather map which Redlands had drawn knowing that it was necessary to explore further but also knowing it was impossible to do so.

From his travel case that he had brought with him he withdrew a pair of binoculars.

On the return trip it was an easy matter to pick out the coaster well ahead of the aircraft, its dark outline contrasting markedly with the pale blueness of the background. There was nothing unusual about the ship, although from this altitude it was difficult to discern close detail, especially as the Widgeon was by no means a good plane from which to carry out such an examination.

'Well?' Fielding asked him.

Ward had no answer to give; he returned the binoculars to his case.

'Just one thing,' Fielding said, 'it's following the same course as we are.'

'Probably going to one of the islands,' Ward replied, a nagging doubt hovering at the back of his brain.

'There's nothing else out here,' Fielding said, 'not a thing.'

'Just the coaster.'

'Yeah — so it must be the coaster — right?'

There was nothing to lose Ward thought. If he returned to Fiji now, the whole thing was over — finished.

'Ten more miles and put it down,' he instructed.

'You're joking.'

'You said it must be the coaster — I'm agreeing with you — now wait until we're a decent distance further on and land or whatever the term is for one of these things at sea.'

Fielding grinned at him, 'Long shot,' he said, moving the controls.

Fifteen minutes later the Widgeon was skimming the sea at sixty five miles an hour waiting for the water to slow the little plane.

The American cut the engines. 'If they don't start again,' he said, 'it's one hell of a long swim.'

'You have a radio, don't you?' Ward asked.

'Sometimes it works, other times it doesn't. I doubt if we could raise anywhere from here with it anyway.'

Ward patted his case which lay on the floor. 'I've got a radio in here,' he said.

Appearing to be unimpressed Fielding left his seat and crawled forwards into the nose where he fiddled with the catches on two small horizontal doors. After a few minutes he managed to fold back the hatches enabling him to stand up with his body protruding through the aperture.

'I'd chuck out an anchor,' he shouted through the windshield at Ward, 'but it's too deep here to ever reach the bottom.'

Ward disappeared aft to collect the

lunch that Fielding's house girl had prepared. The American was back in the cockpit when he returned.

'We won't drift anywhere,' Ward said.

'That's for sure — I've never seen it so damn calm — there's just a swell and a small one at that.'

Ward passed a package of sandwiches and a flask of iced coffee.

'I want to know what the hell we do now,' Fielding said.

'Wait until this afternoon and see if that ship is still on the same course; don't you think it's a bit of a coincidence that it seems to be lined up exactly with the flight path on here?' Ward pointed to the map.

'Pretty thin coincidence,' Fielding said through a mouthful of sandwich.

'If you knew some of the coincidences that have caused me to be here right now you wouldn't say that.'

'Tell me,' Fielding said.

'No — I can't.'

The pilot stretched lazily. 'What could a dirty coaster have to do with all of those air crashes; do you reckon they've got anti-aircraft guns on board or something?'

'I don't know, but I know it's not guns or missiles, none of the planes ever had time to radio for assistance and it's pretty hard to blow a big jet out of the sky when it's maybe forty thousand feet up and moving at six hundred miles an hour.'

Fielding grinned at him. 'A laser,' he said, 'or how about a lariat?'

'It's hard to believe the ship is what we're looking for,' Ward answered, 'but you were right, there's nothing else out here — not that we've seen anyway.'

'It's your money,' Fielding said, preparing himself for a nap. 'Wake me up when it's time for the check.' He closed his eyes.

Ward clambered into the nose of the Widgeon and sat on the edge of the hatchway. It was warm, the ocean being peculiarly free from any wind. Allowing himself to think of Joanne, he wondered if she had yet regained consciousness — it seemed as though he had been away from Los Angeles for a very long time already. His present situation was verging on the comical, he thought; sitting in the middle of bloody nowhere at a hundred dollars an hour, waiting to find out if a nondescript coaster was sailing coincidentally along the route of M.P.173. Even if it was, it certainly didn't prove anything and there was nothing he could do about it.

For the next few hours, Ward occupied himself with what he could only term wild speculation — trying to think of any explanation for the presence of the coaster was an interesting mental exercise, but that was all it probably was, Ward thought — an exercise.

At four o'clock he shook Fielding. 'Let's go and see,' he said, waiting for the pilot to fully wake up.

Fielding helped himself to the remainder of the coffee. 'I've lost my enthusiasm for this,' he said. 'I'd sooner be back on Malolo Lailai.'

He peered vacantly out of the windows. 'Okay,' he said, 'belt up.'

When the Widgeon was airborne, Ward spoke again. 'How about keeping out of sight — if you fly along the line on the map. I'll watch with the binoculars. If I spot it directly ahead again, then she's still on the same course and that'll confirm our suspicions.'

'It's not all that suspicious,' Fielding remarked.

'I know, but I've thought about that for a long time whilst you've been asleep — if the ship's still on the same route as the plane that's due tonight, I'm going to follow my hunch.'

Before Fielding could pass further comment, Ward was shouting excitedly, 'There she is — get down or turn before they see us.'

Ahead, through his glasses, a black dot lay on the surface of the ocean — perhaps the crew on the boat had seen the Widgeon too — there was no way of knowing.

Fielding had banked sharply at Ward's exclamation and was now proceeding in the direction from which they had first approached the ship.

'How about that?' he said with a smile.

Earlier in the afternoon, Ward had decided what he would do if the ship had

161

not altered course. He hoped he could persuade the pilot to help him.

'How fast would that ship be travelling?' he asked Fielding.

'Oh — twelve, maybe fifteen miles per hour — I don't work in knots.'

'And how high will the Widgeon go?'

Fielding thought for a moment. 'I don't know for sure but it could probably reach eighteen thousand feet given long enough — why?'

Ward ignored the question and asked another of his own. 'Will it glide?'

'Every plane will glide, this one will but a bit like the proverbial brick.'

'From eighteen thousand feet with the engines off, how far could we glide then?' Ward asked.

'Christ, I don't know,' Fielding exploded. 'Stop asking stupid questions and tell me what you're thinking about.'

Ward unfolded his map and started scribbling some calculations in one corner of it.

'The Malaysian Pacific D.C.8 will fly over the ship at exactly two twenty a.m. tomorrow morning,' he said. 'Or it will if

162

the ship keeps going at the same speed — if the aircraft is on schedule and if I've got the position of the ship marked correctly on the map. At that time I want to be no more than a mile away and I don't want anyone to know we're there.'

'Good luck,' Fielding said dryly.

Ward continued. 'We have two choices,' he emphasised the word we. 'We can return to the island to refuel and wait for a while before we take off again. You fly well south of the ship whilst climbing to maximum altitude — then, with the engines off, we glide down in the dark so that we get good and close without them seeing or hearing us.'

'Bloody hopeless,' Fielding said rudely. 'First of all, if you stretch your memory back to last night you might remember the moon. Secondly, I've already told you I don't know how far the Widgeon will glide and the chances of judging the distance correctly are pretty slim. Thirdly, on a dead quiet night they'd hear us hit the water with no trouble at all — there'd probably be a bit of phosphorescence in the wake too. Fourthly — '

Ward held up both hands to interrupt. 'Okay, okay, so it's a lousy idea — it'll have to be the other way.'

'I hope it's better than the last one.'

'It is. Listen; we skirt south of them immediately — well south — and overtake them. It's five o'clock now, so in nine and a half hour's time, the D.C.8 will intersect when the ship is another hundred and fourteen miles further on. We'll already be there waiting — on the surface I mean.'

'You've forgotten something,' Fielding said.

'No, I haven't — I know we won't have enough fuel to get back.'

'So we can't do it.'

Ward looked at him sternly. 'Yes we can. We fly back home for as far as we can, then radio for help when we run out. There's no other way — even if we go back now and refuel we still won't have enough to do the round trip.'

'I knew you were mad the first time I met you,' Fielding answered, but from his expression Ward sensed that he might just do what he had asked.

'The only other complication arises from the fact that I've based my calculations on your guess for the speed of the coaster — I used twelve miles an hour. I suppose they could even stop — that'd foul everything up.'

'Stark raving bloody mad,' the American muttered. 'And all because of a hunch.'

'You might as well start now,' Ward said. 'We're flying in the wrong direction and burning up gas all the time.'

Fielding reached beside his seat and produced a bottle. This time it was not Coca Cola. Uncorking it with his teeth, he put the Widgeon into a tight turn before taking a long drink. 'Mr. Nielhart,' he said, 'I hope you know what you're doing; but, as you've already told me that you don't, I suppose I'm being stupidly optimistic.'

Justin Nielhart would have been the first to freely admit that he was acting rashly. In a few hours' time the imprudence of his decision would be dramatically impressed upon him in a way that he could not possibly have imagined.

9

It was unnaturally quiet.

The gentle lapping of the water against the hull of the Widgeon had ceased over an hour ago and now it was as though the aircraft was floating on the mirror-like surface of an inland lake.

'I can't figure it,' Fielding whispered, as though frightened to create any noise that might disturb the stillness of the night. 'I've never known the ocean to be like this — there's no breeze at all.'

'There's still a swell,' Ward said, 'but I suppose it's pretty slight really.'

'The easiest way to see how calm it is,' Fielding said, 'is to look at the swathe of the moonlight on the water — look at it — just as though it was a slick of paint.'

Ward polished the inside of the windshield with his handkerchief for the hundredth time. 'It's a bit creepy somehow,' he said.

'Yeah — it's how it gets before a hurricane starts blowing.'

Thinking back to Los Angeles, Ward wondered if Graham Redlands was still monitoring the weather and following his anticyclone. If he was here now in the middle of the high pressure area, sitting just a few feet above the sea, he would have been gratified to see that his predictions had been so accurate.

Fielding interrupted his train of thought. 'D'you suppose they'll be displaying navigation lights?' he asked.

'I don't know,' Ward said. 'We'll see them coming easily enough if they are.'

'We'll see them in this moonlight anyway.'

'Not if they've changed course or if my calculations were wrong,' Ward said, knowing that the Widgeon could easily be floating many miles away from the correct position.

'If they've changed course the boat has probably nothing to do with the D.C.8 we're expecting,' Fielding replied, lifting Ward's binoculars from the seat.

He peered intently at the horizon,

scanning the glasses over an angle of twenty degrees.

'If we start to drift,' he said, 'we could wind up facing the wrong way to look for the ship — you'd better keep your eye on the compass so as we can paddle ourselves back to the right position if we have to.'

'What's the time?' Ward asked.

Fielding offered no answer, his attention apparently drawn to something he had seen through the binoculars.

'Can you see her?' Ward asked anxiously.

'No,' Fielding answered without moving. 'But I can see something that I've never seen before.'

'What — for Christ's sake, what?' Ward said in a very loud whisper.

Again receiving no answer from the pilot, Ward seized the glasses not able to restrain his curiosity any longer.

'Over there,' Fielding pointed. 'What the hell are they?'

Ward's binoculars had been provided by Military Intelligence. They had a magnification only of seven but a wide field of view and it was only a moment before he had located the subject which had occupied Fielding's interest.

At a distance which he could only guess at, a ghostly white sphere seemed to be climbing upwards from the dark line of the horizon. Illuminated by moonlight and moving very slowly, the ethereal bubble had an almost spectral quality about it, filling Ward with a combination of apprehension and inquisitiveness.

And then, higher in the sky much further away, he saw another. Scanning upwards with the glasses he quickly found one more hanging almost motionless in the night sky whilst in the extreme distance he fancied he could just detect a third.

Fielding was saying something.

'What?' Ward asked, still trying to rationalise his thoughts.

'How many could you see?' Fielding repeated.

'Two — maybe three — I'm not sure.'

'All in a straight line coming towards us?'

Ward nodded.

Fielding appeared nervous. 'I don't like it,' he said. 'And I figure your hunch has turned out to be right after all.'

Knowing his entire trip had definitely not been wasted, but also knowing that here at first hand was part of the answer to the mystery which so many men had been trying desperately to solve, Ward experienced a cold feeling of foreboding. He was sure that the release of these giant bubbles was a prelude to the death of M.P.173.

Fielding took a long pull on his bottle. 'Okay, Mr. Nielhart,' he said, 'what the hell are they?'

Ward had been thinking furiously. He thought he knew what the objects were.

'They're meteorological balloons,' he said, 'I'm sure that's what they are — hydrogen filled met balloons.'

Fielding was unconvinced. 'Do you mean it's just a weather ship letting off those things?' he said.

Ward laughed shortly. 'Not bloody likely,' he said. 'What we've just seen has got something to do with the D.C.8 that's

170

on its way — you can bet on that.'

He consulted his watch. 'Nearly midnight,' he said. 'If the coaster's travelling at twelve miles an hour, she should be about thirty miles away and I don't think we'd be able to see a met balloon that far in the distance — not in moonlight anyway.'

'So you think we're too close?' Fielding asked anxiously.

'I don't know,' Ward replied, 'but I've seen them launch balloons with radio sondes on them. The balloon starts off pretty small in diameter and expands as it gains altitude because the outside air pressure reduces.'

'We could move on a short distance,' Fielding said.

'No, we'll stay here for a while,' Ward picked up the binoculars again.

'Two more,' he said briefly. 'They're letting off a whole string of them.'

The pilot was becoming agitated. 'Look Nielhart,' he said, 'if you're sure those balloons have got something to do with the plane crashes, we can't sit here and let this D.C.8 fly into trouble.'

'We have to,' Ward said. 'I have to be sure.'

'But we could save the lives of all those people.'

'We still might be able to but not yet — anyway, there's over two hours to go,' Ward answered, knowing it was possible that he might have to wait until the bitter end before he had the answer he needed.

His ribs were hurting badly and he was beginning to tense up. Christopher Ward found that he was unable to come to terms with the idea that he might have to decide to sacrifice M.P.173. He was not equipped to act as God — being in the possible control of the destiny of perhaps a hundred and fifty people was something Ward had not been trained to handle. In an attempt to mentally diminish the responsibility that now was placed upon him, he forced himself to recall the projects on air traffic control on which he had worked so long in Europe. Thousands of passengers had unknowingly relied on the electronic systems that Ward had originated in his offices at I.A.S., but somehow this was different — very different. On this occasion, just a few miles away over the horizon, someone had set in motion a deliberate plan to murder a large number of people and Ward was uncomfortably closely associated with the eerie preparations.

'Could we radio the plane?' he said suddenly.

'Yeah — when they get a bit closer — are you going to tell them?'

'I don't know,' Ward said awkwardly, 'I'll have to decide later on.'

'Maybe there won't be time.'

'And maybe I've got it all wrong — I have to know for certain, Fielding — you must understand — I have to know what happens next!'

'Look,' — Fielding pointed through the window of the cockpit.

Noticeably larger than its predecessors, another balloon was soaring skywards in the yellow moonlight. This time there was no need to use the binoculars.

'That coaster must be a lot closer than we thought,' Ward said. 'Can you climb into the nose of the plane and out onto the top? If you stand up outside you might just be able to see the ship with that bit of extra height.'

Ward was right. A few seconds later Fielding was waving excitedly at him. The pilot returned immediately to the cockpit. 'Masthead light,' he said, whispering again as though the sound of his voice would reveal their presence. 'Legally she should be displaying a white light on her foremast — twenty to forty feet above the hull I think.'

Ward made some rapid mental calculations. 'Were you standing up straight out there?' he asked.

'No — nothing to hang on to.'

'The ship's only about ten miles away,' Ward announced. 'If your eyes were five feet above sea level and the light is fifty feet up, she's only ten miles away.'

'We'd better move, Mr. Nielhart — she'll see us for sure — even run us down maybe.'

Ward shook his head pointing to another balloon. 'Not yet — I know it's a lousy way of estimating but that balloon is hardly any closer to us than the last

174

one. I think they've slowed down — might even have stopped.'

But the coaster had not stopped. Two hours and four balloons later the port and starboard lights could be seen quite clearly from the Widgeon, the sinister black outline of the vessel silhouetted against the less dark background of the sky.

Feeling exposed and vulnerable, the two men in the small amphibian had left it too late to leave their chosen position. If Fielding were to start the engines now, detection would be certain. Still believing that the approaching ship was reducing her speed, Ward had persuaded the pilot to keep the Widgeon where she was for too long — a decision he was beginning to regret.

Twelve minutes later, to his immense relief, Ward satisfied himself that the coaster had indeed stopped her engines and was now resting motionless on the surface.

'Now what?' Fielding whispered.

'Ten minutes before the plane's due — there's no doubt that we're onto something,' Ward replied quietly. 'Turn on your radio.'

'Transmit you mean?'

'No, goddam it — receive — I'm not ready to warn them yet.'

'What frequency?' the pilot asked.

'Two one eight two kilo hertz — marine radio frequency — go on quickly.'

Fielding attended to the controls on the radio, wishing with great sincerity that he had not agreed to assist the thin Englishman on this awesome undertaking.

'Are you ready?' Ward snapped, his sense of authority regained now that the long period of waiting was over.

Fielding nodded.

'About ten miles a minute,' Ward muttered. 'It's only eighty miles away — we won't have long — '

His sentence was interrupted by a crackling on the Widgeon's radio.

'Make sure the volume's not too loud, Jack,' Ward instructed. 'They're going to make contact.'

'Surface vessel *Doniambo* to M.P.173 — are you receiving me?' The voice was high, as though spoken by an oriental.

Ward became electrified. This was it — he hadn't failed — at first hand he was about to witness the method used to bring down the big jets. He listened intently as the message was repeated.

Fielding sat in the cockpit of his aircraft, an expression of disbelief stamped across his usually relaxed features.

'M.P.173 to *Doniambo* — go ahead please.' The captain of the D.C.8 confirmed contact with the radio operator on the coaster.

'Please switch to one nine one two kilo hertz — repeat one nine one two,' the peculiar voice lisped out of the speaker on the Widgeon.

'That's a hell of a funny frequency to use,' Fielding said, tuning his instrument in accordance with the instruction.

'This is M.P.173 on one nine one two kilo hertz — what is your message *Doniambo* — over.' The captain of the aircraft sounded bored.

There was a slight pause before the coaster answered. When she did, the airline captain was only marginally more horrified at the communication than the two silent observers in the floating Widgeon.

'*Doniambo* to M.P.173, please listen carefully. From now on, all other frequencies are jammed — you will communicate only on one nine one two and will follow my instructions in order to guarantee the safety of your passengers and crew. Three minutes ahead of you, a single white beam will be directed upwards from my ship. This will be your signal to begin your descent. A flare path will be laid out one mile to the north and you have thirty minutes in which to circle, jettison your surplus fuel and make your approach. Should you choose to ignore these instructions your aircraft will be destroyed in the air with consequential total loss of life. The surface conditions are ideal for a carefully judged landing and I recommend that you elect to be sensible. You may advise your passengers and crew that a forced landing will be necessary. We are standing by.'

'My God,' Ward breathed, unprepared for the content of the transmission.

Fielding was dumbfounded, unable to speak.

Equally unsuspecting, the disconcerted and frightened captain of M.P.173 did not answer for several seconds.

Ward and Fielding listened anxiously for both the sound of the approaching aircraft and the reply that the captain would give to the *Doniambo*.

'M.P.173 to *Doniambo* — go to hell you bastard, you're not getting me like the others and I'll be back with some friends to fix you up later.' There was commendable fierceness in the reply from the pilot of the jet aircraft.

A pure white light beam licked up from the deck of the coaster, thrusting coldly towards the sky. Almost simultaneously, three extremely bright balls of fire flared along the flight path high in the stratosphere.

'*Doniambo* to M.P.173 — suggest you comply or suffer certain destruction.'

'The balloons,' Ward exclaimed, suddenly understanding. 'They've set a complete network of them at the right altitude.'

In the distance, about three miles behind the coaster, a further series of orange flares burst over the calm Pacific, the faint thud of the explosions reaching the Widgeon much later.

'Must be bloody great bangs for us to hear them at all — they're forty thousand feet up and a few miles away,' Fielding commented. 'I wonder what the captain's going to do.'

'M.P.173 to *Doniambo* — okay, let's have your surface lights — I have a hundred and thirty eight people up here and I can't seem to outrun your artillery — will you guarantee our safety if I get this bird down in one piece?'

The answer came quickly from the operator on the coaster. 'Certainly captain — now please hurry.'

Ward turned to the pilot of the amphibian. 'This is the sixth aircraft these bastards have brought down and as far as we know, no passengers or crew members have ever survived — we've got to do something — I've got all the information

I want — I shouldn't have waited so damn long.'

A high pitched buzz filled the cockpit of the Widgeon as Fielding tested the other frequencies. 'All jammed completely,' he said, 'they must have real powerful equipment to do that. We can't radio for help, even if we were in range of any receiving station.'

Tormented by the knowledge that he was about to actually see the D.C. super 8 attempt a dangerous landing on the ocean whilst he was powerless to act, Ward became erect in his seat.

'I can't let it happen, Jack — all those people on the plane — no one will ever see them again — just like the others.'

Then, ahead and to the left of the Widgeon, he saw the launch. It was moving extremely quickly, the noise of its exhaust drifting over the sea towards the amphibian. At a speed that Ward estimated must be nearly sixty miles an hour, with a beautiful rooster tail spraying from the stern, it streaked north. Almost at once the roar from the powerful motor seemed to fill the night.

Behind the launch a series of red lights bobbed in the wake where they had been dropped overboard to form what was quite obviously to be the flare path. Turning at the end of its run in a curve of white water without reducing speed, it sped back to lay another row of burning flares some three hundred feet away from the first line. When it had completed its task, the skipper throttled back before changing his course in order to return to his mother ship.

Meanwhile, the coaster had extinguished her searchlight and lay waiting like a spider for the fly she had enticed into her waiting web.

Fascinated, the two men in the amphibian watched the red lights increase in brightness covering the whole area in a weird glow of crimson smoke.

Ward seemed to be frozen in the cockpit, stunned and horrified at the scene before him. Jack Fielding had lost his nervousness, being no longer aghast at the prospect of watching a large number of people risk their lives at the instruction of the radio operator on board the

Doniambo. He had decided that he must act.

'Those balloons,' he said suddenly, 'do you figure they just had high explosives hanging from them — or would it be more complicated than that?'

Ward pulled himself together. 'I don't know — they could be H.E. warheads, or more likely giant fireworks so that they couldn't damage the plane — it's obvious they want it down in one piece.'

'But the explosives, whatever they are, do they just hang there at the right altitude, or are they released from higher up, or even guided?'

There was urgency in Fielding's voice.

'How would I know,' Ward answered desperately.

The pilot began to fasten his seat belt.

'What are you going to do?' Ward said in surprise.

'Get the hell out of here and tell the captain of that plane to keep going — we can transmit to him on the same frequency as that big bastard. Now you strap yourself in real tight and use the radio while I fly this old lady out of the road — here grab this.' Fielding thrust the microphone into Ward's hand.

The pilot punched the starter for his port engine, waiting for it to fire cleanly before starting the other. Without waiting for them to warm up Fielding opened the throttles wide making the Widgeon shudder as it began to move.

At once, the launch that had been nestling alongside the coaster burst into life, the familiar rooster tail curving out as it accelerated towards the Widgeon. This time, the savage roar from the fuel injected Continentals on the wing above the cockpit drowned the note of the rapidly approaching launch.

Fielding had seen the movement and was swinging the Widgeon away as the little amphibian gained vital take-off speed. 'They'll never catch us,' he yelled to Ward, who was preparing to transmit. 'P.D.3 to M.P.173,' Ward shouted into the microphone, using the first call sign that came to mind. 'Can you hear me?'

The captain's voice crackled from the speaker immediately. 'M.P.173 to P.D.3

whoever you are — go ahead.'

Guessing that the operator on the *Doniambo* would try and block the exchange, Ward made his message brief.

'Execute evasive manoeuvres and get the hell off your normal flight path,' he shouted above the engine noise. 'They can't hit you if you veer away and we suspect those fire balls are just for effect — now go for your life.'

There was the merest pause before the confused airline captain answered.

'Thank you P.D.3 but you're just too late, I have already completed dumping my fuel — please advise alternative.'

'Bloody hell,' Ward howled to his own pilot. 'Now what?'

Needing another ten miles an hour before the Widgeon reached the magic sixty five, Fielding was totally absorbed in the task of taking off whilst simultaneously attempting to decide whether or not it was a machine-gun that was flashing from the bow of the pursuing launch.

A loud buzzing sounded from the radio confirming that the *Doniambo* had extended their jamming to all frequencies, and the cabin of the Widgeon suddenly became flooded with dazzling radiance as the coaster picked out the fleeing amphibian with its powerful searchlight.

The *Doniambo* lay directly behind the Widgeon as Fielding finally lifted off, making it difficult for Ward to see the launch.

'They're firing at us,' Fielding yelled, pushing the plane into a sharp turn almost immediately after leaving its creamy wake on the surface of the Pacific. 'Keep your fingers crossed, Nielhart — and your legs too.'

Observing the high frequency flashes stabbing up from the skimming launch below, Christopher Ward knew that they were going to be lucky to escape. He was very frightened indeed.

But now that the Widgeon was free from the drag of the water, the little plane began to open the gap, Fielding keeping his engines wide open, meanwhile executing violent swoops from what felt like one side of the world to the other.

As if realising that the race was lost, the launch turned in a cloud of spray leaving the amphibian to continue with its withdrawal. 'They've given up,' Ward shouted, but his relief was to be short lived.

A mile behind, illuminated by the evil red glow from the flares, the D.C.8 was coming in — a huge and harmless bird snared by the diabolic black coaster that had accounted for five other similar aircraft.

Three square miles of unusually placid ocean was in turmoil as men concentrated on a variety of critical tests of skill. On board the coaster, two carefully picked men moved the sights of twin twenty millimetre Oerlikon anti-aircraft heavy machine-guns. With loving sensitivity, they centred the concentric rings over the silhouette of the fleeing Widgeon. It was almost too simple.

Aware that they had failed totally in their efforts to save the D.C.8 and its innocent unknowing passengers, but believing that the men who had perpetrated these hideous accidents would now be brought to trial when the truth became known, both Fielding and Ward were watching the jet aircraft plough into the sea. Fielding had swung the amphibian parallel to the lines of the red flares in order to observe the landing, secure in the knowledge that the launch had abandoned the unequal pursuit of the faster airborne Widgeon. If he had continued to fly away from the coaster and if he had continued with the clumsy evasion technique which he had adopted when being fired upon, there would perhaps have been a remote chance that he could have escaped. Instead, the first burst from one of the Oerlikons smashed violently through the tailplane of the fragile amphibian, cutting the controls and carrying away a portion of the rudder.

Horror struck at the sudden noise, cold fear swept through the pilot as the flashes from the rear of the coaster appeared again. Beside Fielding, Christopher Ward felt his stomach heave with the sickening revelation that they were under fire.

Appalled at his stupidity, Fielding

wrenched at his useless flight controls, already knowing that his plane was stricken.

More twenty millimetre shells tore huge gaping holes in the nacelle of the starboard engine, disintegrating the crankcase and rupturing the fuel lines. Flames immediately licked rearwards over the single wing, intensifying as the flying wreckage of the plane began the dreadful spiral into the sea.

Pitilessly, the Oerlikons followed the flaming remains, blasting part of the fuselage away before the elevation angle became too low for them to continue with the destruction.

In a series of crazy, irregular twists, the doomed amphibian corkscrewed downwards, occasionally appearing to flatten its suicidal descent into the water which it had left such a few minutes before.

The end was unimpressive. Still burning, what was left of the Widgeon hit the water with one wing tip, a final forward swoop when the plane was no more than ten feet above the sea slowing the downward velocity and transferring the energy instead into horizontal motion. The wreckage executed two cartwheels before it came finally to rest.

A mile and a half away from the coaster *Doniambo*, the Widgeon continued to burn for several minutes before the cool water extinguished the fire for ever.

Closer to the ship that had destroyed the helpless amphibian, surrounded by burning flares, the big Douglas jet was suffering a more gradual death.

10

Forty years ago, an enthusiastic and unusually gifted group of aircraft engineers had met in the New York offices of the Grumman Aircraft Corporation to establish the basic operating parameters of the Widgeon amphibious plane. In order to satisfy the requirements for a low take-off and landing speed it had been necessary to provide a wingspan of forty feet which, for a small plane having an overall length of only thirty two feet, was not only generous but gave the Widgeon certain other valuable attributes. It was perhaps for this reason that the little amphibian was destined to become so successful.

One of the characteristics possessed by the Grumman Widgeon is its ability to respond quickly to small changes in forward speed, the wing section being able to provide significant lift to the airframe under conditions when a more modern, swifter aircraft might well be quite unstable.

Whether or not the brief respite from the twirling dive allowed the Widgeon to make one vain attempt to save itself from violent impact with the water, will never be known. Perhaps the American pilot, who had chosen to live his life in the friendly islands, made one final desperate effort to regain control of the plane that had served him so well for many easy years. Whatever it was that caused the transient pause in the spin, it had allowed the two occupants of the doomed aircraft to escape with their lives. How long they would continue to survive was a question of some doubt.

Terrified, sick and dizzy, Fielding had resigned himself to his death shortly after losing control of his plane, knowing that the impact would either drive the shattered remains of the Widgeon deep beneath the sea or squash the frail fuselage to crush the occupants. Christopher Ward had also given up all hope of survival and had been astonished to find that his fear had given way to an objective appraisal of his life in the few seconds that were left to him.

When the Widgeon flattened out, its hull momentarily parallel with the tranquil surface of the moonlit Pacific, Fielding had seized his chance. Years of flying had allowed him, at least to a small degree, to retain a sense of direction throughout the spin and the pilot knew that for a very, very short while the remains of the plane were going to glide. Using automatic reflexes, he unbuckled his belt and leapt to the door.

Fielding hit the sea on his back at fifty miles an hour, his body bouncing with devastating roughness. Arms and legs flailing, battered from the impact, the pilot had come to rest in a flurry of water in time to see the Widgeon's wing-tip slice knife-like into the sea. Knowing that the plane would sink at once with its fuselage ripped open by the machine-guns, and thinking that Nielhart would be lucky not to die from the spreading flames before he drowned, Fielding had begun to swim towards the wreckage.

As soon as the cartwheeling had

ceased, feeling as though every bone in his body had been broken, Ward had just had sufficient presence of mind to unfasten his seat belt before the acrid fumes from the fire made it impossible for him to continue breathing. Too confused and too concussed to fight for the oxygen that would keep him alive for another few precious seconds, he had quickly become unconscious.

Flames had enveloped the cockpit by the time Fielding reached the wreckage. Had he not been saturated with sea water, he would never have been able to have hauled himself back into the blazing aircraft. As it was, the pilot's hair was alight before he had managed to man-handle Ward's limp body through the door.

Badly burned, Fielding had pulled the man he had rescued away from the heat, wondering if he was already dead and wondering if it was going to make any difference one way or the other.

The Widgeon had sunk shortly afterwards, the water extinguishing the flames as each part of the plane slid hissing beneath the surface.

That had taken place nearly ten minutes ago and now, his entire body feeling as though it was on fire, Fielding knew that he would be unable to support the man he had saved for more than another few minutes.

But the cold water had been working on Ward. He regained consciousness as though awaking from a nightmare, as indeed he was. Not knowing what had happened, he struck out, inadvertently swallowing two mouthfuls of sea water. The spluttering and subsequent coughing caused him to gasp in pain, for his partially healed ribs had not been capable of withstanding the ordeal that he had so narrowly survived.

Free of the deadweight of Ward, Fielding turned onto his back to float. He was not able to speak until he had recovered some of his remaining energy.

'Another minute,' he said, speaking between burnt lips, 'and I'd have let you drown.'

Ward swam painfully to the man who had saved him, not fully aware of how he came to be still alive.

'Are you all right?' he asked.

'No — pretty burnt I think — all I can feel is fire — had to pull you out.'

Ward turned his head towards the ship. Still illuminated by the flares, the D.C. super 8 was floating quietly amidst what appeared to be a good deal of flotsam. With his eyes only inches from the surface, Ward was not able to see if passengers were leaving from the escape hatches and the familiar agonising pain from his ribs made it difficult for him to concentrate on anything other than keeping alive.

Further in the distance, the coaster was ablaze with light, a strange contrast with the ship that Ward had been watching earlier in the night. Men were shouting to each other and the noise of several engines carried across the water.

'Nielhart,' the pilot moaned, 'what the hell do we do now?'

'You've been asking me the same damn question ever since we left Fiji,' Ward replied in a strained voice, 'and I keep on giving you the same answer — I don't bloody well know — how about drowning?' It was a feeble attempt at humour in a situation where the technique could not possibly achieve the desired effect.

Fielding spat out a mouthful of water. 'Maybe it'd stop the pain, but I'll hold on for a bit yet thanks,' — but his voice was strained and it had cost him dearly to answer at all.

Ward thought of the life jacket that he had carried in his case — if there had been time to grab it perhaps both of them could have remained afloat for several hours. But the case and the life jacket had sunk with the wreckage of the Widgeon and Ward knew that inside half an hour both men would be dead. If one of them had escaped uninjured and if one single buoyant fragment of the broken aircraft had stayed floating within easy reach — then and only then, would there have been a slight chance of them surviving. There were too many ifs — Ward and Fielding were as good as dead.

Supported by the gentle ocean, each man was left to his own thoughts, wondering how much longer he was prepared to fight against the inevitable.

In fact, less than twenty minutes had elapsed when Ward suddenly became aware of an approaching boat. Moving very slowly, it was the launch that had laid the flare path.

'Jack — Fielding, can you hear me?' Ward gasped.

There was an answering groan from the pilot.

Knowing that this would be their only chance, Ward drew on his final reserves. Feeling as though his chest would explode, he gave one mighty shout whilst lifting one arm in the air. Had he known how pitifully weak his cry had been, Christopher Ward would have let himself slide under, knowing that he had failed.

But Ward had not failed. Miraculously, his pathetic attempt to attract attention had succeeded. The launch pointed her sharp bow towards the two bobbing heads and increased her speed.

A broken and exhausted Englishman was dragged from the sea, to be followed by an equally insensible American his face distorted by scalding pain from the burns that covered his face and limbs.

The launch turned back to the floodlit coaster, skirting the still floating Douglas jet now much lower in the water. In the bilges of the launch, barely aware that they had been snatched from their graves, two men lay numb and motionless in a sodden heap.

An hour and a half later there was no flotsam to mark the scene of two air disasters. A tiny slick of oil marked the position where the Widgeon had landed for the last time, but the much larger aircraft had left nothing to show that it had perished here.

Sailing due north, the coaster disappeared into the emptiness of the Pacific, her mission successfully accomplished.

★   ★   ★

When the weather broke four days later, the ship was much closer to the equator, making conditions in the raised poop even more intolerable. In the tiny cabin in which Ward and Fielding had been imprisoned, the temperature had risen until now it was in the region of one hundred degrees Fahrenheit, and in the rougher sea it was proving almost impossible for the two men to leave their bunks with any safety.

Both had received crude medical treatment, the burns of the pilot having responded well to the applied salve that still covered his face and hands; Ward was bandaged again, the fractured ends of his broken ribs being pulled rudely into place once more. The oppressive heat had done little to help the condition of either man, perspiration feeling like rivers of acid to Fielding whilst Ward's absorbent bandage had become quickly saturated to rub his flesh raw across his chest and back.

Three modest meals had been brought to them on each day of their confinement, and a Japanese doctor or the medical attendant on board the coaster had visited the prisoners on odd occasions.

For the first two days there had been little or no exchange of conversation between the two men. Then, as the pain reduced and the stunned shock of their experience slowly faded, it had been possible for them to spend an increasing proportion of their time in open speculation. What had happened to the passengers of M.P.173? Why had the *Doniambo* dispatched the launch to search for survivors from the Widgeon? Where was the coaster bound for now? To these and fifty other questions they had no answers.

It was not until the morning of the fourth day that the two men were given the opportunity to satisfy their curiosity.

The Polynesian, who Fielding had said was probably of Nukuoroau extraction, delivered breakfast as usual — some smoked meat, a slice of bread for each man and a huge mug of black coffee which they had to share. When he returned to collect the tray he held open the door motioning that they should follow him.

More commonly known as a short-sea trader, the vessel that had identified herself as the *Doniambo* had a gross tonnage of nine hundred and eighty and was a little over two hundred and thirty feet in length. Built in Britain in 1959 she had operated in the Baltic and the North Sea before coming south to the warm seas of the Pacific. With a raised quarter deck several feet higher than the well deck, she was typical of her vintage, a useful all purpose cargo carrier but one that had been adapted for a particular job. The bridge and accommodation for the crew were located well aft and it was only necessary for Ward and Fielding to climb one companionway before they arrived at their destination. An open steel door swung on its hinges as the ship rolled in the heavy swell.

Their escort appeared unwilling to enter the cabin, but made it plain that he wished the two men to go in. Fielding followed Ward through the door.

Inside, a small gnarled Japanese gentleman in his late fifties stood behind a simple steel desk. He wore black horn rimmed spectacles of tinted glass, the heaviness of them dwarfing his miniature features. Sunlight from a single circular porthole combined with the yellow glow from a dirty bulb in the ceiling to provide a level of illumination that was hardly adequate. The harshness of the steel lined cabin was relieved by a huge coloured chart of the South Pacific, interlaminated in clear plastic and fixed to the bulkhead that faced the door. A single chair behind the desk completed the rudimentary furnishing.

Once Ward and Fielding were inside, the door was closed behind them leaving them alone with the strange little man. He sat down.

'Gentlemen,' he said in perfect English. 'If I may say so, you are extremely fortunate to be alive — may I ask if there were others in the plane that were less lucky?'

'Does it matter?' Fielding answered with a controlled edge to his voice.

'Not in the slightest — you must forgive my curiosity though — I saw your aircraft crash and understandably find it remarkable that anyone survived.'

'How many people survived from the D.C.8?' Fielding said angrily.

The Japanese held up a hand. 'I will answer your questions when and if I see fit,' he said. 'You are here to answer questions that I will ask you — you were rescued for that specific purpose.'

Sensing that Fielding's approach could cut short the interview prematurely, Ward decided that he should become the spokesman for both of them.

'You sent your launch to search for survivors from our plane,' he said. 'Why did you bother?'

The thin lips of the elderly Japanese compressed as if to smile. 'That is a more interesting question,' he said. 'My answer will perhaps allow you to guess why I ordered a search to be made. Whilst engaged with M.P.173, having previously given the instruction for your aircraft to be destroyed, it was brought to my attention that you used a most peculiar call sign at the start of your radio message — you may remember it perhaps.'

'What's he talking about?' Fielding said.

With the beginnings of an explanation dawning in his mind, Ward recalled his abortive attempt to advise the captain of the jet. 'P.D.3,' he said slowly, 'I used P.D.3.'

The man behind the desk nodded. 'Indeed you did, you identified yourself with Pacific Disaster Investigation team three — an offshoot of I.A.S. and an organisation with which I am not entirely unfamiliar.'

'How do you know about it?' Ward asked, believing that he already knew the answer.

The man behind the desk displayed obvious irritation. 'I have already explained that you are not here to waste my time by asking questions.'

Fielding appeared to become equally annoyed at what he quite obviously considered to be the unreasonable attitude of the diminutive Japanese. He moved towards the desk and leant forward.

'Look,' he said, 'as far as I'm concerned, you are a murdering bastard and you can stuff your questions little yellow man. Sure you rescued us — after you shot down my plane — so bloody what? I figure that any answers you might get from Mr. Nielhart here will only help you bring down another jet, so you can throw us over the side of your lousy ship and forget about the questions.'

Unmoved by Fielding's blunt statement, the man removed his glasses to polish them with some tissue he took from his desk. He seemed unaffected by the rolling of the ship.

'My name is Goro Shiga,' he said, 'I am Japanese. Perhaps my name might be known to you.'

'And my name's Jack Fielding — and I know bloody well you've never heard of me.'

Shiga ignored the pilot. 'Although born in Japan, I have been unable to live there since the termination of World War Two. I am fourth on the list of men wanted by the American Government for war crimes, Mr. Fielding — I am an exile from the more populated parts of this world and I am a very cruel man. Whether or not you choose to co-operate now is of little consequence — you will answer my questions eventually — I guarantee it, Mr. Fielding — I guarantee it.'

This time Fielding had no reply. He

moved back from the desk, staggering to keep his balance as the coaster lurched in the heavy sea.

There was a cold feeling in Ward's stomach. Although not entirely surprised to discover that the men responsible for the air disasters were merciless killers, the revelation that he was the prisoner of a self-confessed war criminal was nevertheless somewhat frightening to the Englishman.

'Perhaps you could obtain any information that you think we might possess more easily if, in return, you could satisfy some of our curiosity,' he said. 'But I can assure you that we know nothing whatever of any interest to you.'

'It is not necessarily I who wish for an explanation of your presence in the M.P.173 zone,' Shiga said. 'However, it would be advantageous if I were to have at least a rudimentary report prepared before I return. If, as you say, you know nothing, then your answers cannot possibly benefit me — but I regret that I must still have them. However, I am prepared to discuss the matter reasonably if this interview can be terminated more quickly by doing so. I have no real objections, because of course any information that you might gain will be of no subsequent use to you.'

'Why?' Ward said bluntly.

The Japanese stared at him. 'Because you are dead men — once you have been interrogated again at our base, you will be executed — I am sure you must understand that.'

The statement was said without expression, a cold condemnation to death. Ward shuddered inwardly. They wanted to know how much he knew and then, when they had found out, he would be killed — but apparently not until the ship reached home, wherever that was. He wondered how many hours he had left.

It was not difficult for Christopher Ward to reach a decision; he knew nothing of any real significance and to lie could serve no useful purpose. It would be better to try and learn what he could and hope that an opportunity to escape would present itself later. The knowledge that escape would in all probability be impossible, did not alter anything.

'You mentioned P.D.3,' Ward said.

Shiga shook his head. 'You mentioned it on the radio — if you had not you would be dead already.'

'But you know about the P.D. projects?'

'Yes, we know of them all, and we know that results of the investigations have been valueless — what chance do stupid men stand against some of the finest brains in the world. P.D.3 did, I understand, begin to establish a pattern that could have made it necessary for us to modify our methods — we obtained a tape recording from Los Angeles from one of our men — it was not difficult to monitor progress on any of the P.D. projects.'

'Who was your spy?' Ward asked.

'Just the janitor, Mr. Ward, an unobtrusive and inexpensive informant.'

Ward started at the use of his name.

'How do — ?' he began, only to be interrupted by Fielding.

'You don't even know his name,' the pilot sneered. 'Just a bloody guess.'

Shiga compressed his lips again. 'What have you to say to that, Christopher Ward, project co-ordinator of P.D.3?'

'You recognised my voice from the tape,' Ward said slowly.

'You mean your name's not Nielhart?' Fielding asked, confused and with his suspicion aroused.

'My name's Ward — I used to run P.D.3,' Ward answered the American wearily. 'This Japanese gentleman organised an unpleasant plan to kill me and my assistant when we were working in L.A. — needless to say he failed.'

'And what has happened to P.D.3?' Shiga said, 'whilst you have been flying around the Pacific with Mr. Fielding?'

'Colonel Douglas has taken over,' Ward lied.

'Don't lie to me, Mr. Ward — you are not a stupid man and, if you think for just a moment, you will conclude that my informants will naturally still be working. We cannot afford to be complacent — we are not stupid either.'

'Is the *Doniambo* the headquarters?' Ward said.

A faint smile flickered transiently across the impassive face of Goro Shiga.

'This ship is not our headquarters,' he said, 'and she is not the *Doniambo*. The *Doniambo* will be a thousand miles away by this time.'

'But you identified yourself as the *Doniambo*,' Fielding said.

Shiga inspected the back of his tiny hands as if searching for a wrinkle that he had not seen before.

'It is necessary to make contact with the aircraft on an internationally accepted radio frequency — otherwise it is possible that our initial transmission might not be received. As a precaution, we adopt the name of the vessel that is closest to our operating zone. The *Doniambo* is a merchant ship operating out of New Caledonia; at the time that we first spoke to M.P.173 she lay one hundred and six miles to the south — her progress had been plotted for some days before. As I am sure you will appreciate, should anyone have been fortunate enough to have picked up our first signal, it is possible that a search will have been mounted for the *Doniambo*. When they find her they will be as confused as her

211

innocent captain. You doubtless heard that the aircraft is subsequently instructed to reply on another most unusual frequency whilst we jam all others with our powerful radio equipment. From that time onwards only very low power transmissions are broadcast from my boat. It is a simple method of deception — possibly unnecessary, but we regard it as inexpensive insurance. Naturally we do not discount the remote chance of encountering an airline captain who decides that he will make a bid to escape from our balloon system. With each successive plane, the chance increases — I understand the airlines are becoming desperate. Should a plane manage to slip through our fingers, it is most advantageous to be identified with a vessel that has absolutely no connection with us.'

It was a remarkably simple ploy; Fielding and Ward exchanged glances.

'So what is the ship?' Ward asked.

'She is a pirate ship, Mr. Ward, an innocuous coaster designed to prey on the rich aircraft that cross the Pacific. For minimum financial outlay we have been able to collect a very substantial quantity of negotiable currency and other most valuable commodities. The exercise is also one of considerable interest — it has never been attempted before. At my age the novelty has much attraction.'

Fielding exploded. 'Novelty,' he yelled, 'what about all those people — where are they for God's sake, where are they?'

Shiga blinked at the pilot through the thick lenses of his spectacles, his wrinkled face still impassive.

'It depends on your religious beliefs,' he said. 'Some people would suppose that the passengers are in heaven — or in hell perhaps. In my own mind, I am certain only that they are at the bottom of the ocean still inside their aircraft. Canned sardines, Mr. Fielding, as my crew call them.'

The Japanese man neatly anticipated the pilot's next move. A large automatic appeared in his hand. 'I dislike hysterics, Mr. Fielding, and I have little interest in the information that can be extracted from you — do not be foolish.'

'You insane bastard,' Fielding shouted,

'you're a monster — a dehumanised evil bloody monster,' — but he had not lost his control and knew that his life was worth nothing to the Japanese with the gun.

Ward remained silent.

Goro Shiga placed the automatic on the desk top. 'I am not — and the group of men that I work with are not — dehumanised, as you put it. Rather we are concerned with easy profit that we have elected to obtain by unique methods; whether or not people die as a consequence is of no significance to us. Passengers on the aircraft are killed painlessly by inducing large quantities of nerve gas into the cabins as soon as the plane is at rest on the water. We have five well equipped launches that inject the gas through holes that are punched in the fuselage, invariably long before the hatches are open from inside. It is an easy way to die, gentlemen.'

'And then you plunder the aircraft?' Ward asked, the final pieces of the jigsaw beginning to fit into place.

'Hard currency, frequently valuable

cargo, drugs, cameras and other expensive similar equipment, personal goods, clothes and liquor.' Shiga ticked off the items on his fingers. 'We average a hundred thousand American dollars for a 707 originating from the United States.'

'But what about some of the other flights?' Ward asked. 'F.I.003 from Noumea to Suva and A.A.961 were half empty.'

'Ah, Mr. Ward, that is more complicated. If we can predict suitable weather conditions — I regret that the balloons and our surface activities require perfect weather as you know — then we can arrange for certain cargoes to be placed upon chosen aircraft for collection when they are brought down. In some instances, drug smugglers fly with their contraband and we reap the benefit — you were close to the truth with your ingenious statistics, Christopher Ward.'

'And when you have collected the loot?' This time it was Fielding who asked the question, his anger moderated by listening to the elderly Japanese man describing the reasons behind the murder of some hundreds of people.

Shiga consulted his watch. 'I have to radio to my home base shortly,' he said. 'There may be further opportunity for you to discuss my organisation, but now, Mr. Ward, I must insist that you bring me up to date with P.D.3. I did not expect to be able to question you personally — it is a most unexpected pleasure.'

'Just one more short question,' Ward said.

'What is it?'

'Where are we being taken, Shiga?'

'To Truk, Mr. Ward, an eight hundred square mile island filled lagoon in a rarely visited part of the Pacific Ocean, a former Japanese naval command headquarters and my home since the end of the war — now please begin with a resumé of the work carried out by you and Miss Varick in Los Angeles. I am sure you will not be so stupid as to distort the truth.'

There was nothing to be gained either by lying or by refusing to co-operate. With Jack Fielding listening intently, Christopher Ward began at the beginning of the project that had finally led to his capture on board this evil ship. Not only had he failed in his mission, but in a few days' time he would be as dead as the passengers on board the planes he had tried to save.

11

Ralph Douglas slammed down the telephone receiver with such violence that the whole desk trembled. If there had been someone within audible range he could perhaps have vented some of his rage and frustration by bellowing at them, but the office was empty and the Colonel was once again conscious of being particularly alone.

One light burned in the two top floors of the El Segundo building, a solitary bulb to illuminate the only office still in use on the defunct project that had been known as P.D.3. Not even the impersonal computing equipment remained, for machines of such great cost could not be allowed to stay idle for very long. Yesterday, the last member of the maintenance staff had left and the computers had been moved to a new installation where there was new work to be done.

Quite alone in the deserted building, Douglas stared out of the window towards the air terminal two miles away. With landing lights blazing, the big aircraft were making their final approaches, lining up with glowing eyes like so many giant moths that had been attracted to the thousands of lights that are L.A. by night.

Four days ago, P.D.3 had officially ceased to exist and since then the skeleton team that had been made responsible for tying up the not inconsiderable number of loose ends had steadily reduced in number. Four days had also elapsed since M.P.173 had first been reported missing.

Still looking out of the window, Douglas thought of his abortive struggle to use his final days in searching for the answer that P.D.3 had been unable to find quickly enough. Now he too had suffered ignominious defeat. He had embarked upon a single handed wild goose chase that had fizzled out already. He was finished, his career ruined.

Shortly after Christopher Ward had left

Los Angeles, Colonel Douglas had spent several uneasy hours in conversation with Graham Redlands during which he had convinced himself that he had acted irresponsibly in assisting the young Englishman in his quest to discover the truth at first hand. Then, after the safe arrival of Ward's aircraft in Fiji, Douglas had managed to shed the burden of his conscience for a short while. It had not been until Redlands had phoned him at the hotel on the following evening that his anxiety returned. The anxiety had quickly turned to a definite feeling that he was neglecting his duty in remaining inactive when three intelligent men believed that M.P.173 was earmarked for catastrophe. The Colonel had decided to compromise and wage a one-manned investigation of his own.

Using his not inconsiderable influence, Douglas had contrived a plan that would allow the progress of M.P.173 to be monitored from the time that the aircraft had left Singapore. The international radio stations which lay along the route to Djakarta and onwards to Darwin and

Mexico were asked to maintain a full listening alert. All communications were to be relayed at once to the Colonel who would be sitting in the centre of the miniature special purpose network that he had created. Douglas had significantly overstepped the accepted boundaries of his authority but believed that the risk to his future was now necessary. At the very worst, he had thought, he would be discharged from Military Intelligence and Douglas knew that at his age it was about time he started to consider retirement be it voluntary or otherwise. Anyway, young Ward should be provided with some backup — just in case help was needed. It was the least the Colonel could do.

As Redlands had pointed out, all evidence was in favour of M.P.173 being the sixth aircraft to disappear; if he was right, the prospects for Colonel Douglas would indeed be bright. And so Douglas had taken the risk. It had so very nearly paid off.

On his desk lay a tape recording, the meaningful part of which lasted for precisely eighteen seconds — he had timed it very carefully. It contained the initial exchange of conversation that had taken place between the captain of M.P.173 and the vessel *Doniambo* — all transmitted on the conventional frequency of two thousand one hundred and eighty two kilo hertz. The remainder of the tape was of no use, being made up of a series of unpleasant bursts of radio interference interlaced with short passages of barely recognisable speech where ground based air traffic controllers had tried in vain to make further contact with both plane and ship on a variety of other frequencies.

Awful indecision had prevented Douglas from acting immediately. Unable to be sure that what he had heard had been the beginning of something he did not and could not understand, he had waited for five hours before contacting the U.S.A.F. base at Guam.

A search for the vessel *Doniambo* had eventually been mounted after a great deal of argument with Air Force chiefs of staff, not only in the Pacific but in the United States itself. The Colonel had been forced to account for the unauthorised expenditure of nearly two thousand dollars and had been severely reprimanded for the extremely irresponsible way in which he had elected to continue a project that had already been cancelled. Stubbornly refusing to be intimidated, Douglas had staked his reputation on eighteen seconds of recorded speech.

It had taken rather longer to find the *Doniambo* than anyone had anticipated. Only two aircraft were used, the low priority assigned to the search being the result of the Colonel's inability to completely convince the necessary authorities of the seriousness of his theory. When at last the New Caledonian merchant ship had been located and ordered to stand by, Douglas had experienced a premonition of his downfall.

Returning home after receiving the information that her mission had been called off, one of the Australian frigates of P.D.1 had been dispatched to intercept the waiting *Doniambo*. It had been the official report on the status of the merchant vessel that Douglas had received a few minutes ago by telephone.

There would be no future for him now. He reached again for the phone to call Graham Redlands and tell him the news.

* * *

Stretching like a coral necklace across more than three million square miles of the western Pacific Ocean, the islands of Micronesia bear some of the deepest scars of World War Two. Over two thousand specks of land wind down through vast reaches of open sea, extending for thirteen hundred miles from north to south and nearly twice that distance from east to west.

Because the land mass totals only nine hundred square miles, Micronesia is an ideal location for any vessel wishing to hide itself from the eyes of the world and, even in the nineteen seventies, there are an astounding number of uninhabited islands that are rarely if ever visited.

For many years, a number of the larger island groups were off limits to tourists

224

and even after restrictions were lifted it was still extraordinarily difficult to travel to them. Then in 1968, Air Micronesia began flying into the area from Honolulu and development and tourism were soon under way.

Guam, Saipan, Yap, Majuro, Truk and many others — islands that would stir the memories of many Pacific war veterans — all became instantly accessible to the inquisitive and wealthy American tourist. But Micronesia still remains an area of great solitude and it has yet to be spoilt by the coarse commercialism that spreads like a disease across the world. Of all the major island groups that are well known, Truk is perhaps the one which modern civilisation has touched the least.

A collection of verdant hills rising high from a huge lagoon measuring forty miles from reef to reef at its widest, Truk is a fairyland of incredible beauty. Once it was not so, for Truk was the mightiest naval installation built by the Japanese Imperial Fleet outside of the Japanese homeland; but the base did not spoil Truk for very long. Today, below the surface of the tranquil lagoon, the wreckage of more than sixty naval ships give silent testimony to the success of the surprise bombing attack carried out in February 1944. Since that time, on the land, the jungle has recovered her own.

Six days had elapsed since the coaster had snared M.P.173 and now, as she sailed through the south pass of the Truk reef, it was as if she had come home to rejoin her sunken friends of long ago.

The magnificent scenery would have been of little interest to the two men imprisoned on the ship even if they had been able to see it, which they most certainly could not. Still held captive below decks, Christopher Ward and Jack Fielding, whilst recovering from the injuries that they had sustained from the crash of the Widgeon, were now ill from the awful heat and sick with fear of their uncertain future.

Yesterday, they had been interviewed by Shiga again for the whole of the afternoon and the old Japanese had repeated the cold sentence of death that he had mentioned at their first meeting.

Ward and Fielding had learnt more about the way that this sinister organisation operated, but their new found knowledge had done little to raise their hopes of finding an opportunity to escape.

Goro Shiga was the operation's commander for the short sea trader that was used to bring down the jet aircraft. Supporting him was a team of men based in Truk. The uncanny parallel with the exploits of pirates who had operated in another century from Caribbean islands had been discussed at length between the two captured men.

Three ex members of the Japanese Imperial Navy were responsible for establishing the entire enterprise, all of them war criminals who had evaded capture by the American authorities at the cessation of hostilities at the end of the war in the Pacific. Understandably the men were no longer young and Ward had found it difficult to imagine how they could still wish to wage effective war against the airlines and the world public at such an advanced age.

Shiga had given the impression that the

reasons behind the operation were principally financial, although there was no doubt that the challenge of the foul undertaking was appealing to all of the people associated with it.

A year ago, a number of wanted men that had been living secretly in the islands of Micronesia for nearly thirty years had come together to form a project which was as ingenious as the one that Christopher Ward had led in Los Angeles.

Using Truk as their operating base, a complete system had been originated, equipment manufactured and local native support staff recruited to assist on board the coaster and on the small island where the headquarters had been established. Substantial sums of money had been spent in setting up distribution channels for the goods stolen from the aircraft, whilst an elaborate chain of agents had been installed in almost every major country in the western world. These were men who were able to arrange for huge quantities of drugs to be smuggled on board aircraft that had been selected for extinction. Knowing that the customary search carried out at all international air terminals would quickly reveal even small amounts of narcotics on arrival at their destination, it was simpler to recover the material at sea once it had been successfully exported from the country of origin. From then onwards the complex distribution system would take over.

Two methods of disposing of the rich plunder were employed. The first of these was by direct transfer of selected commodities from the coaster to equally innocuous small ships that pre-arranged to rendezvous in mid-ocean. The other method, which was reserved exclusively for high price items and all drug traffic, relied on buyers travelling especially to Truk to collect the merchandise that had been previously ordered. Wanted for atrocities committed three decades ago, three men had established a Pacific trading post for some of the most wanted products of this sick earth.

To the astonishment of Ward and Fielding, they had discovered that it was not only aircraft that were robbed of everything they carried. Private yachts, large launches and even freighters were targets for the brilliantly equipped black coaster. Not able to conceive of piracy on this scale, the authorities had neglected to consider that so many lives were being lost because of one small group of evil and greedy men. Men, women and children had been cruelly murdered for the value of the goods they carried. It was trade in death and dollars on a terrible scale.

Shiga had admitted that it would not be possible for his organisation to continue their activities for an indefinite period. Eventual detection would be inevitable — especially if they continued to concentrate their efforts in the Pacific. Furthermore, there was the very real risk that one of the aircraft would one day escape from the balloon system.

Carrying ten pounds of plastic explosive connected to a radio controlled detonator that could be triggered when required by a signal from the ship, each hydrogen filled balloon was pre-set to hover at precisely the correct altitude in order to intercept the target aircraft. The warheads were quite harmless but extremely spectacular and it was easy to understand how dramatic their effect would be upon frightened airline captains.

Other systems in comparison would be expensive and probably less efficient. Conventional anti-aircraft guns would have little chance of achieving the desired end when dealing with a target moving at five hundred miles an hour at an altitude of thirty thousand feet in the dark.

Nevertheless, it was easy for the balloons to move off course under the action of stratospheric winds that were difficult to detect prior to launch. The balloon network was the weak link, Shiga had explained, requiring much improvement. Already, four shipments of drugs had been missed because the weather had changed unpredictably between the time that the instruction had been given to smuggle them on board a particular plane and the time of interception with the ship. The rapid communications around the world that were necessary for the system to operate relied on coded radio messages and Shiga feared the time when some enthusiastic cryptologist would stumble upon the secret of Truk. But the men at Truk had other plans for the future that Shiga had not divulged — Ward did not doubt for a moment that they would be as sinister and as successful as the ones used on the present project.

It was midday by the time the coaster had safely negotiated the passage into the shelter of the lagoon, the swell of the open sea reducing at once. For the past two days the weather had been overcast and the ocean somewhat rough; now, only a few miles from home, the sky showed signs of brightening, the grey giving way to whiter fluffy clouds through which occasional patches of blue sky could be seen. Soaked in perspiration and dehydrated from their days of confinement in the hot airless cabin, the two prisoners became aware that the sickening rolling of the ship had stopped at last.

'We must have passed through the reef,' Fielding said.

With his face set against the pain that he knew must accompany the movement,

Ward lifted himself from his bunk. 'I thought you said you'd never been to Truk?' he said.

The American shook his head. 'I haven't,' he said. 'But I know it's got a reef all round it — Truk isn't one island — I think there are a hundred of them — all inside a big lagoon. Shiga said so.'

A noticeable change in the vibration from the diesel in the engine room below seemed to confirm Fielding's belief.

'I wonder how long we'll have?' Ward said, broaching a subject that they had so far avoided talking about.

'What, before we reach their base?'

'No, I didn't mean that.'

The pilot looked at him. 'I don't know, Chris — but sure as hell I'm going to make it hard for them.' There was a hard edge to his voice that Ward had not heard before.

'You said there were villages on the islands,' Ward said. 'If we can make a break for it could we get to one, or don't you think that'd do us any good?'

Fielding thought for a moment. 'I'm pretty certain there's a tourist resort on

Moen,' he said. 'There'll be Europeans there for sure — even tourists — but I don't know enough about the geography of the place to know how to find Moen.'

'What about the other islands?' Ward asked.

'Native villages I expect — probably only speak Micronesian or bastard Malay but they might help us I suppose — but we've got to get to one first, Chris.'

Knowing that he was incapable of any strenuous physical effort in his present condition, Ward doubted that either he or Fielding would be able to travel very far. Any escape attempt that they might make would have to be carefully planned; it would be senseless to consider fighting their way out, even if an opportunity were to present itself.

There was a further detectable reduction in engine speed. A moment later the steel door to their prison swung open.

Goro Shiga stood outside.

He squinted through his glasses at the two men. 'Good afternoon,' he said. 'If you would be kind enough to accompany me to the bridge you will be able to enjoy some fresh air and see something of Truk.'

Although Shiga spoke perfect English and was almost too careful in the way that he chose his words, there was no courtesy either in his manner or in the bland expression on his wrinkled face. Now Ward knew him better, it was easy to see through the superficially pleasant exterior of the Japanese to the cold and heartless old man that lay beneath. Ward and Fielding were to Shiga as meat animals to a farmer — it was not difficult for the Englishman or his friend to sense the impersonality in Shiga, despite his polite invitation to join him on the bridge.

The clean fresh air was wonderful. The ship was still moving, the resultant breeze acting like a tonic upon the men who had been forced to stay below deck for six days. In the daylight, both of them presented a sorry sight — Ward's bandaged trunk making him appear almost grotesque to the American pilot. The burns to Fielding's face had not been serious, leaving the skin raw and peeling, but his legs and arms were covered with open suppurating lesions that were hardly less painful than they had been five days ago. Surprisingly, Ward's small beard had survived the fire in the cockpit of the Widgeon, only having been singed on one side — indeed, it was possible that the beard had protected his face from the flames. The ex project leader of P.D.3 was perhaps a little more gaunt and more pale than usual. In contrast, Jack Fielding had grown an untidy eighth of an inch of dark bristle on his scorched face.

They looked at each other, the pilot managing a wry smile.

'You look like hell in that bandage,' he said. 'Why don't you take it off and see if you fall to pieces?'

'I'll collapse,' Ward assured him. 'If you knew how it felt to have yourself held together with this piece of sweat soaked material, you wouldn't even think that I liked wearing it.'

Shiga waved expansively at the magnificent spectacle before them. 'It is a pleasant place — do you not think so?'

There was more blue sky now and the sun had been able to penetrate the cloud in several places, turning the sea to a pale green. Islands were everywhere, their shorelines punctuated with jungle filled valleys and ravines between which lay ragged coastlines of bays, beaches and rocky cliffs. Occasionally, savannah-like expanses could be seen and here and there on palm shaded promontories, clusters of low profile buildings showed where a village had been built.

In no mood to be impressed by the tropical scenery that he had lived amidst for the last six years, Fielding wanted to know where they were headed.

'To Dublon island,' Shiga answered the pilot's question. 'A former Japanese command headquarters — we will be there soon.'

He pointed ahead between two other larger islands. 'You can see it already.'

'Where's Moen?' Ward asked, thinking that the information might be useful to have.

'Moen is about two and a half miles further north from Dublon,' Shiga said. 'To port is Fefan and to starboard Uman. The little one to the right of Dublon there is Eten — does that satisfy your geographic curiosity, Mr. Ward?'

Surprised at the number of small boats that were dotted about the big lagoon, Ward began to think that their chances of obtaining assistance, if they could escape, would be rather better than he had anticipated.

A huge trimaran flying an unknown flag passed by the port bow of the coaster. Shiga raised a hand to the people on board. 'That is the tour boat from Moen,' he explained. 'It remains inside the reef which is undoubtedly wise — I have no faith in three-hulled boats.'

'There seem to be plenty of people about,' Fielding remarked to no one in particular, although Ward knew that the message was intended for him.

Shiga answered. 'I believe the population exceeds thirty thousand for the entire island group — many of them are our friends. Our enterprise supports two entire villages on Dublon, as you will see.'

Looking for the first time at the well deck of the short-sea trader, Ward could see some of the special purpose equipment with which she was fitted. Everything was painted black including the five powerful launches that lay clamped into steel cradles welded to the deck plates. There was a derrick for each of the launches giving the ship the appearance of being cluttered, but everything was well maintained and clean and tidy.

On the raised forecastle a black tarpaulin covered what Ward supposed were the heavy anti-aircraft guns that had been used to destroy the helpless Widgeon, but there was no sign of any machine-guns mounted on the bows of the launches.

They were close enough to Dublon now to pick out a palm fringed inlet that the coaster was heading for.

'You will return below with this man,' Shiga instructed. 'It is necessary for us to manoeuvre the ship into our mooring system and I anticipate that both of you may decide to make a final bid to save your lives. A natural enough reaction, but one that cannot possibly succeed. I do not wish to have to contend with your stupidity whilst dropping anchor.'

As large and young as Shiga was frail and old, a Japanese sailor took hold of Fielding to escort him back to the cabin. Despite his injuries and his harmless appearance, the American pilot was dangerous to manhandle. Earlier, he had hinted to Ward that he had chosen to live his life on the island of Malolo Lailai as the result of an unfortunate offence he had committed years before in the United States, and now Ward realised that the American was made of sterner stuff than he could have ever imagined.

Relaxing as if to be led by the man who had seized Fielding's wrist, the pilot suddenly sprang forwards and spun round in one easy motion. Then, almost faster than the eye could see, he executed three wicked chops with the edge of his right hand. As the Japanese began to fold forwards at his waist, Fielding accelerated the motion by placing his hands behind the neck of the already partially senseless man and pulling with all his strength. When the unprotected head was three feet from the floor of the bridge, the American appeared to leap in the air with both legs bent. With terrible violence his knees smashed into the face of the sailor, shattering the bones in the cheeks and crushing the frontal portion of the skull just above the nose. Death was instantaneous, the victim of the shocking onslaught collapsing onto the deck, a pool of blood forming around his head.

Hardly able to believe that Fielding was capable of making such an extraordinarily brutal attack, Ward stood rooted to the ground unable to speak.

The pilot seemed unconcerned by the fact that he had killed a member of Shiga's crew. He said quietly, 'You miserable little bastards, if anyone touches me again I'll kill them too — I don't like it.'

Goro Shiga moved his head forwards as if in a slight nod. Expertly wielded with just sufficient force, the butt of an automatic crashed onto the back of Fielding's skull. He crumpled into a heap. The sailor who had responded to Shiga's silent instruction rotated the gun in his hand until the muzzle pointed at the centre of Ward's bandaged stomach.

'You will not die easily,' Shiga spoke to the unconscious pilot as though he could hear what was being said. 'You will pay for your stupidity, Mr. Jack Fielding, and I will wait until you scream to be killed before I end the pain.'

Three minutes later, Ward was thrown back into his cell, the limp body of the American being dragged in afterwards where it was dropped unceremoniously upon the floor.

Frightened more of being left to die alone at the hands of his captors than of death itself, Ward directed his attention to reviving the pilot.

On the bridge, annoyed that one of his men had been needlessly killed but without experiencing a trace of compassion, Shiga began to prepare his ship for the homecoming.

Half a mile from the dark green island, the launches were lifted off their cradles before being swung outboard and lowered in readiness for the numerous trips that they would have to make to the mouth of the estuary where the cargo would be finally unloaded. Below decks, the crew started to free the crates that contained the spoil from I.A.885 and M.P.173. Empty hydrogen cylinders and empty cylinders which had contained deadly nerve gas were withdrawn from their racks in the hold, whilst some of the more complicated radio equipment was carefully demounted from the operations room in the poop so that it could be transferred to shore for checking.

And all the time, the rest of the world was mourning the loss of yet another aircraft without knowing that as long as Truk retained her secret, the destruction and murder would go on.

12

It was evening before the launches had finished ferrying their plunder to the shore, the huge orange ball that was the dying sun hanging low over Dublon island.

Accompanied by Shiga and four armed guards, Ward and Fielding were the last to leave the coaster. To Ward's relief the American pilot had recovered consciousness shortly after being dumped into the cabin and was now suffering only from a nasty headache, although the rough treatment he had received had done little to help the painful burns that scarred his limbs.

Each launch was powered by twin Chevrolet V.8 engines converted to marine use and at their operating speed of four thousand revs per minute, over four hundred and fifty horse-power was available at the shaft of the single outdrive unit. Designed specifically to operate in conditions of almost dead calm with a very shallow Vee to the black glass fibre hulls, it was not surprising that the launches were usually able to administer their deadly injections to hapless aircraft before the fuselage hatches were removed by their flight crews.

Hardly seeming to touch the water, the launch sped towards the shadow of the inlet, the familiar roar from the exhausts seeming to Christopher Ward as though it was heralding the final act of the awful drama that he had become part of.

Half a minute later the throttles were eased back as the jungle covered slopes of a natural estuary rushed to meet them. At reduced speed the launch nosed her way deeper into the curving waterway until the lush vegetation on the banks seemed to exclude all light from the fading sun. The inlet progressively narrowed causing the man at the helm to use an occasional burst from the engines in order to maintain his chosen course. Then, after rounding a gradual left hand sweep, the banks receded to encompass a larger expanse of green water and the launch had reached her destination.

Floating quietly alongside a short wooden jetty the other four launches that had preceded them were being unloaded. A mixture of Japanese and native islanders had formed a human conveyor stretching from the wharf to the still laden boats, whilst a Toyota Land Cruiser was being piled high with boxes and crates by another smaller team of men.

All work stopped as the prisoners from the last launch disembarked. Dressed only in loin cloths and with open lips parted in betel nut red grins, the islanders stared at the new arrivals. The Japanese members of Shiga's land based organisation appeared equally curious, but wore surly expressions as Ward and Fielding were escorted past them on their way to the waiting vehicle.

A quick glance around the wharf revealed the remains of a number of concrete buildings almost completely obscured by jungle, and two derelict gun emplacements also nearly hidden by the dense green foliage of tropical flora.

Without having time to properly absorb all that he had seen, Ward was bundled after Fielding into the Land Cruiser where he had to find space to sit amongst the other freight. Sufficient room remained for only one of the guards, a man who had obviously been warned to take no chances with the two prisoners. He sat on a cardboard box moving the muzzle of his gun first towards one of them and then to the other.

'Where do you think we're being taken?' Fielding asked.

Ward had questioned Shiga about his headquarters briefly whilst on their way from the coaster, receiving the impression that it was located close to the point of unloading.

'I don't know,' he said. 'Maybe they're going to take us to the place where they're going to kill us.'

'We've been brought all this way just so as someone here can talk to you personally before they bump us off.' Fielding said. 'I don't think we're that close to the end yet.'

'Do you suppose Shiga's boss refused to accept a report from him about us?' Ward queried.

'Maybe they have another reason for wanting us here, Chris.'

'No, I don't think so — Shiga was telling us the truth — he had no reason to lie — the people here — the other two Japs that run things probably want to satisfy themselves that I've told Shiga everything I know about progress on P.D.3; it'd be pretty important for them to find out exactly.'

The Land Cruiser's motor started and at once the vehicle began to move away from the wharf, travelling along an extremely bumpy and overgrown track that soon began to climb steeply upwards along the precipitous bank of the estuary.

There were occasional glimpses of more gun emplacements, and here and there more rusting remains of the Japanese war machine could be seen in the jungle as they passed by clearings that had still not yet been totally enveloped by the creeping vegetation.

After travelling for not more than a

mile, during which the gradient seemed to remain remarkably constant, Ward and Fielding sensed that they must be nearing the end of their journey. The quality of the road improved and the Land Cruiser began to overtake odd pedestrians who waved excitedly to the driver. Then, in a cloud of swirling dust, the vehicle crested the ridge of the valley and accelerated towards a group of buildings that huddled at the end of a grass covered air strip. Many years ago the top of the ridge had been bulldozed to provide a long and narrow tract of relatively flat land for the Zero fighters that had been based here. Although the jungle had reclaimed much of the ground, some two thousand feet of usable grass still stretched along the artificially created plateau and there was evidence that attempts were being made to cut back more of the encroaching undergrowth at the far end of the runway.

The Toyota pulled to a stop outside a corrugated iron structure that had been recently fitted with large windows, fly screens and venetian blinds, giving it a most unusual appearance. Ward and

Fielding climbed out, apprehensive of the welcome that they might receive. But they were not permitted to enter, their watchful guard leaning against the wall with the gun still trained upon them as if he was waiting for something.

Unwilling to talk to each other, Ward and Fielding watched some men that materialised from a nearby thatched hut unload the Land Cruiser before it turned round to disappear in the direction from which it had come.

'Gone to fetch the others,' Ward remarked.

Fielding nodded at their guard. 'D'you figure he speaks English?'

'No, I doubt it.'

'So how about we jump him right now?'

Ward looked at the nearly naked islanders who, having finished their work for a moment, were squatting comfortably on the grass beside the building.

'If we manage to avoid getting shot,' he said, 'I have a feeling we wouldn't even make the end of the airstrip — our friends here look pretty fit and they aren't covered in burns and haven't got fragile ribs.'

'Anyway,' Fielding said, 'that Toyota will be back soon — I guess we should wait — there's nowhere to run to at the moment either.'

Ward was pointing upwards.

Coming in to land in the rapidly encroaching dusk, a small single engined monoplane could just be discerned against the purple sky.

There was still the vestige of a breeze and from where they were standing it was easy to see the pilot trimming the aircraft to make sure that he avoided a last minute side slip which, on such a narrow strip of grass, would undoubtedly prove fatal.

The plane bounced once creating a miniature whirlwind of dust before slowing down. It taxied noisily towards the group of men.

Shortly before the pilot cut his engines the Land Cruiser returned, this time carrying Goro Shiga in the passenger seat.

With remarkable agility for a man of

his years, he jumped from the cab to speak quickly to the guard. As the result of his instruction Ward and Fielding were shoved into the corrugated iron shed and hurried along a panelled corridor to a small windowless room. There, they were pushed roughly inside with the barrel of the automatic, Fielding starting to snarl at the treatment. But, before the situation had time to develop further, a solid wooden door slammed shut behind them followed by the sound of a bolt being slid firmly home.

No sooner had the two men groped their way around the walls of the unlit room than the characteristic beating of a helicopter reverberated through the walls of their new prison.

'Chopper,' Fielding announced unnecessarily.

'It all seems to be happening now Shiga's back home,' Ward remarked. 'I wonder who's arriving?'

'Let's not stay and find out.'

Ward kicked the wooden lining on the walls. 'You going to eat your way out?' he said rudely.

252

Fielding's voice sounded strained. 'Look, Chris,' he said, 'we're going to be killed — get that into your head — it might be tomorrow, it might be in ten minutes time after they've asked you their questions — every minute we're here we are a little closer to dying — we have to think of escape for every precious second that's left to us — for Christ's sake get your clever brain going — you've got a degree so use it!'

'You can't think your way out of a room with no windows and a locked door,' Ward said helplessly. 'What the hell do you want me to do?'

Before the American could reply the door was thrown open to admit Goro Shiga. He carried a large hurricane lantern filling the room with an intense white light. Accompanying him were two much larger men both armed with sub-machine guns.

'You will sit on the floor,' he said sharply.

Partially blinded and dreadfully frightened that Fielding's estimate of ten minutes was about to prove true, Ward obeyed the instruction at once. He was joined by the pilot who had taken a few seconds to weigh up the odds before moving.

Shiga looked down at the men. 'We have two important customers,' he said. 'They have arrived by aircraft to collect a consignment of heroin that was ordered some months ago. Tomorrow a small freighter will berth here to trade for the cameras — we have over five hundred to dispose of at present. Because we are going to be unusually busy, my two colleagues will not have time to interrogate you for several days.'

Ward's heart leapt — that was better, at least there was time for him to collect his thoughts. But his hopes were to be dashed by Shiga's next remark.

'They consider that the information you may still have will not add materially to what we already know of the stupid and ineffective attempts which have been made to find us. You are only a little fish, Ward, and they are probably right in thinking that we have wasted too much time on you already.'

Ward said nothing, waiting for the Japanese to continue.

'You will be executed at dawn, Christopher Ward — your colleague will follow you later. Mr. Fielding will be given to three of my men who will derive a great deal of pleasure in making him die slowly. I regret that other more pressing business will prevent me from attending either of your deaths. I have seen perhaps a thousand men die in my life, but I still find each one interesting to observe — it is a pity I shall be elsewhere.'

Ward shuddered. The little man was a monster, for nearly thirty years his evil had persisted and the world authorities had probably abandoned the futile search for Goro Shiga long ago.

And now Christopher Ward, scientist, mathematician and systems analyst, was going to lose his life at the hands of this vile creature — and for what? Dublon island would continue to spawn the hell that Shiga and his friends had established here — more aircraft would vanish, more innocent passengers would die without ever knowing why and a thousand people would destroy themselves with the drugs that were distributed from this awful place. A tiny part of a tiny island, lying jewel-like in the great Pacific, was the centre of a cancer that would spread further and further until Shiga and his kind were brought to justice.

The American pilot was equally frightened. To have stumbled upon this nest of snakes by the merest chance of fate was going to cost him his life and Jack Fielding was not yet ready to die. He resolved that he would not allow Shiga's men to torture him first. If he could not escape he would try his best to kill himself.

'You are both very quiet,' Shiga whispered, his eyes owl-like behind his spectacles.

Ward endeavoured to pull himself together. 'How is it that you can operate your business from here?' he said unsteadily. 'There must be tourists who come to Dublon, and Truk itself is not exactly an unknown place, is it?'

'We have a good anchorage for our ship, shelter for our launches, a source of cheap labour, an air strip and the use of many buildings here — we chose Dublon very carefully, Mr. Ward. There are many uninhabited islands or atolls that we could use, but our activities at such places would possibly attract more suspicion than here at Truk. Besides, there is a pleasant hotel on Moen, a well equipped store and other trappings of modern civilisation. It is possible to live there most comfortably as well as meeting a variety of entertaining people. Does that answer your question?'

Ward nodded — 'You don't live here then?'

'No, Mr. Ward, this is our warehouse facility primarily — the islanders look after it very well and we in turn look after them very well — it is an admirable arrangement.'

'Why kill us?' Ward said suddenly.

Shiga turned to leave. 'A stupid question,' he said. 'Goodbye, Mr. Ward, and goodbye, Mr. Fielding — I trust you will spend a pleasant night.'

'You filthy little bastard,' Fielding spat, starting to rise from the floor.

The guards waited until he was on his feet.

Before the American could move forwards, the blunt muzzles of the sub-machine guns sank viciously into his stomach. Retching and writhing with pain, Fielding collapsed on top of Ward causing him to wince from the racking of his own injured ribs. For the second time in two days the pilot had brought down a savage attack upon himself.

There was the familiar thin lipped smile on the face of the old Japanese as he closed the door.

'You bloody fool,' Ward shouted reproachfully at the pilot, 'what the hell was the use of that?'

Fielding groaned in the dark unable to answer.

Ward found a corner of the room to support his back and forced himself to think. Visions of Joanne Varick and his old office in London mingled with impossible schemes for escape. He had a few hours to live or a few hours in which to make a bid for freedom — if he was still here when the sun's first rays turned Dublon

258

from grey to green, Christopher Ward would perish at the hands of his executioners. Almost angrily he pushed his memories of Joanne to one side — she was in a coma and Ward was as good as dead, his existence terminated at thirty two — it was a horrible conclusion to a promising life and the Englishman could not come to terms with the idea.

Ten minutes elapsed before Fielding had regained his wind and until the fierce pain had reduced to the point where he could speak. 'Don't just sit there,' he croaked, 'start digging.'

Ward placed the palms of his hands on the cool concrete base of their cell. 'Are you still lying on the floor?' he asked.

'Yeah.'

'What's it made of?'

The pilot did not answer the question.

Ward banged his fist experimentally on the wall. 'Have you still got your knife?' he said.

'No.'

'Did you see the ceiling when Shiga had the light in here?'

Fielding thought for a moment. 'Hell,

no I didn't,' he said.

Ward groped his way across to him in the dark. 'Lift me up on your shoulders,' he said, 'we've got to try, Jack — there isn't any other way out of here.'

But no possible escape could be made through the solid planks that lined the roof. The effort of maintaining an upright position whilst balancing on top of Fielding's staggering frame cost Ward dearly and he was not able to speak when the pilot returned him to the ground. Fielding himself was gasping with the strain, the bruised muscles in his stomach feeling as though they were being torn apart.

'Bloody hopeless,' Ward said when he had recovered.

'They're not stupid, Chris — Shiga wouldn't have put us in here if he thought we could get out.'

'So we're going to have to think of something else, aren't we,' Ward said, knowing that he had no ideas to offer.

'If we can't get out of here before morning there isn't anything else,' Fielding replied bluntly.

Fighting the dreadful feeling of despair that Ward knew would overwhelm him if he allowed his will to weaken, he tried to rationalise the situation. Escape was impossible from this room and tomorrow he would die — it was no easy matter for him to reason under such circumstances. Any plan for survival that he might formulate would be surrounded with unknowns; for him to predict a pattern of events would be a virtual impossibility, but Christopher Ward was going to try. If he failed he would pay with his life.

In his best boardroom voice, the Englishman began to talk to the American pilot. He was to continue talking for the remainder of the night.

13

Most of the islands in Micronesia share a common climate. Tropical and hot with average humidities that make the temperature seem artificially high prevail for much of the year and rainfall is generally confined to the wet season commencing in July. As a result of this, an easy life style has been developed by the people who live there.

The indigenous inhabitants of these islands are thought to have originated in south-east Asia as long ago as 1500 B.C. They are a fine race of people that easily survived the massive Japanese colonisation during the last world war, although the imprint of Asian influence understandably has not yet been totally erased. In the two native villages near the air strip, Goro Shiga and his compatriots had made quite sure that islanders would continue to regard the three Japanese war criminals as their masters.

Shiga had exerted firm control over the small population, providing them with many luxuries in return for their services. Medicine was available from the buildings that were occupied by a few Japanese who lived near the airstrip, and it was unnecessary for many of the islanders to rely on or trade with the field trip vessel run by the district centre of the trust territory.

To say that the inhabitants of Dublon had become lazy under the Shiga regime would perhaps be an overstatement — but that they had become apathetic was undoubtedly true. The Japanese labourers who worked for Shiga and lived at the airstrip had been culled from a number of undesirable Asians that can be found in any bar in the islands and without exception, they were sullen, ignorant men.

Thus, when dawn broke over the hills of Dublon, it was a collection of disinterested islanders that had gathered to watch the execution of the tall thin Englishman at the corner of the jungle. Whilst the torture of the American pilot with the burns might hold more promise, past experience with captured drug traders had shown that the victims of the stupid Japanese labourers invariably died before revealing their secrets. On this occasion none of the boss men from Moen were to be in attendance and there was a remote chance that there might be more fun than usual.

Before leaving Dublon by helicopter the evening before to entertain his visitors on Moen, Shiga had left clear instructions for the execution of the two prisoners. He would return briefly one hour after daybreak to make sure that the job had been carried out successfully. It was because Shiga was a careful man that he had been able to evade the vast net which had been cast by the Americans to catch convicted war criminals.

As the result of a night of debauchery with seven young island girls — a not uncommon occurrence at the airstrip settlement — the two Japanese guards that had previously assaulted Fielding with their gun barrels were nearly three quarters of an hour late in climbing from their bunks. Knowing that there would be no acceptable excuse for any delay in the proceedings, they hurried at once to collect their victims, pausing only to check the magazines on their Masden sub-machine guns.

The two prisoners were a sorry sight when they were escorted from the crude building, their hair wet and matted from perspiration and their faces displaying undisguised fear. A foul smell of urine and unwashed bodies hung about them causing even the guards, who were none too clean themselves, to grimace briefly at each other. At gun point, the trembling men stumbled from the doorway with eyes squinting in the early morning light. Shielding their faces from the sun they peered stupidly about them waiting for directions.

One of the guards said something in Japanese but failed to obtain any reaction from the trembling captives. Prodding Ward in his broken ribs made the Englishman stagger forwards in the wrong direction, and it became obvious that the prisoners would either have to be dragged to the edge of the clearing where the spectators were waiting or steered there like sick cattle.

Conscious of the fact that they would have to hurry if the job was to be completed before Shiga arrived, both guards placed the short barrels of their guns in the backs of the two men and began to shove.

The American was heard to groan what seemed to be a number as he shuffled his feet forward. Instantaneously a miraculous transformation seemed to overcome the captives. With incredible speed they turned in unison, one hand pushing away the guns the others balled into fists that exploded into the faces of the unsuspecting guards.

On his toes, with a machine-gun in his hand, Fielding pressed home his attack reversing the weapon to use the steel side of the breech as a club. Without mercy he beat the Japanese to his knees before kicking him savagely in the face.

Ward was having more trouble with his man. Aware that he had been fooled by the appearance of the prisoners and

266

knowing that the thin Englishman was fighting for his life, the guard had made a valiant effort to retain his machine gun winding the shoulder strap several times around his wrist. Struggling face to face for possession of the weapon, Ward was beginning to weaken when Fielding opened fire.

Designed in Denmark at the end of the last war, the Masden sub-machine gun has a rate of fire in excess of five hundred rounds per minute. With a weight of seven pounds and an extended length of thirty one inches, it is easily manoeuvrable in conditions of close combat and, at a range of three feet, Fielding had wasted no time in swinging the muzzle round and squeezing the trigger.

His body cut in two at the waist from the single burst, Ward's assailant was hurled backwards by the impact of the bullets, a terrible scream torn from his lips.

Leaving Ward to disentangle the gun from the dead guard, the pilot swung round to face the group of islanders in the clearing. Uncertain as to what to do and confused at the dramatic change in the behaviour of the prisoners, some disappeared quickly into the jungle leaving others standing motionless knowing that they would be cut down if they dared to move towards the fierce American.

Then, faintly at first, but increasing in volume by the second, the chopping of the returning helicopter began to drift across the island.

'Leave it, Chris,' Fielding shouted, 'and go for your life for number four.'

Christopher Ward had spent the entire night creating a series of hypothetical situations. Painstakingly he had outlined in fine detail a variety of circumstances that he believed could confront the two men on the morning of their execution. Taking each one in turn and assigning a number to it, he had discussed the means by which escape might be possible if luck was on their side. He had forced Fielding to argue with him, he had invented more plausible situations than the pilot could ever have believed would exist and had originated, with Fielding's assistance, a getaway solution for each one of them. By midnight, Fielding was almost dizzy from trying to keep up with the fertile imagination of the man from I.A.S. and had at last realised that the mind of Christopher Ward was not the mind of an ordinary individual at all. Twenty three different and definite possibilities had been laid down by the systems analyst and he had insisted that Fielding remember every single one together with the appropriate plan for escape that they had agreed upon for each of the possibilities. It was an exercise in logical thinking and in problem solving that Ward had never before attempted but, throughout the long night, he had been haunted by the knowledge that the technique could not hope to cover every eventuality and could thus easily prove worthless when the time came for them to act.

Nevertheless, the crude system had served them well in the first violent phase of their bid for freedom and as Ward began to run, his confidence in his own ability slowly returned to him.

It had been Fielding's idea that they should appear dishevelled and exhibit signs that they had accepted the inevitability of their death in order to lure the guards into a false sense of security. There was no doubt that the ploy had aided their escape considerably, but already Ward felt he might well turn out to be as physically resigned as the man he had attempted to portray.

Fifty yards away, the light aircraft that had arrived the night before stood unguarded on the runway. Plan four — the number that Fielding had shouted — relied on both men reaching the plane fifteen seconds ahead of any pursuer, but Ward had not foreseen the possibility of the return of the helicopter. Had he known that but for the laziness of the Japanese guards he could have been sprinting along the runway nearly an hour before the scheduled arrival of the helicopter, the Englishman would have cursed his misfortune and perhaps have lost his faith in the system that he had worked upon so hard.

Shortly after he had commenced

running there was another short burst of machine-gun fire. Ward turned to see the bloody corpse of the second guard twitch upon a patch of red grass. Deciding to take no chances before starting his own dash to the plane, Fielding had killed the other man who was to have executed Ward.

With the splintered ends of his ribs sending excruciating waves of pain up and down his chest, Ward approached the green and white painted aircraft. It was a Cessna 150, one of the most popular examples of single engined personal aeroplanes. He reached the door beneath the wing at the same time as Fielding. Both men were gasping from the exertion.

'Give me the gun,' Ward said. 'I'll wait outside until you get it started.'

Fielding swung himself into the cock-pit. 'Believe it or not,' he coughed, 'I need it to start the engine unless you've got a knife or something.'

Like an angry dragonfly the helicopter soared over the belt of jungle at the far end of the runway where it hovered

271

momentarily above the bodies of the dead guards. Several islanders rushed towards it pointing in the direction of the Cessna.

'I'm going to need the gun in five seconds, Jack,' Ward yelled as the helicopter began to tilt towards him.

Lying on his stomach half in and half out of the plane, the pilot was struggling to hold the Masden in the correct position. Closing his eyes he fired a half-second burst at something behind the instrument panel, the bullets penetrating the floor of the cockpit and burying themselves deeply into the dusty soil. He inspected his work and tossed the gun across to Ward.

'Now pray,' he instructed, climbing into the seat.

Still accelerating, the helicopter was approaching quickly now.

Ward sprang to one side of the Cessna, steadied the tubular stock of the Masden on his shoulder and opened fire.

Horribly vulnerable in the plexiglass dome of the helicopter, the pilot had seen Ward before he commenced firing. Wrenching at the controls he lifted his machine in time to miss the lethal stream of bullets.

Ward caught a brief glimpse of Goro Shiga sitting dwarflike next to the pilot before the helicopter whistled overhead in a rapid climb.

Smoke puffed from the exhausts on the Cessna and Fielding was shouting to Ward to get in. Soon the engine was firing smoothly on all cylinders causing Ward and Fielding to exchange glances of disbelief — now, if only their luck would hold, their chances of survival were better than at any time since the Widgeon had been shot down.

Because most engines of small aircraft are fitted with magnetos — usually two — in order to turn off the power it is necessary to earth each of the magnetos through a braided cable connected to the ignition switch. It was this cable that Fielding had severed using the sub-machine gun. Looking at the large rent in the floor as the pilot wrenched open the throttle, Ward could not help wondering if any vital part of the aircraft had been smashed by the bullets.

But the engine revs increased and the little plane began to move. Providing the controls were still intact — freedom was only moments away.

Bouncing along the runway, which was proving a good deal rougher than it had appeared, the Cessna gained valuable speed eating up the length of flat grass at an alarming rate.

The pilot spared a quick glance at his companion. 'It's okay, Chris,' he shouted above the noise, 'we'll be off in seven hundred feet.'

Through the windshield, Ward saw the helicopter execute a fast turn some distance ahead of them. Then, for the first time, he noticed the peculiar framework that spanned the two skids beneath the clear plastic bubble. Fielding had seen it too. He pulled back on the stick and the Cessna leapt from the ground its nose pointing skywards at a dangerously steep angle.

'They've got a gun fixed to the skids,' he yelled to Ward.

'Get ready with yours — smash it through the window before you fire.'

In fact the helicopter had been fitted with two machine guns, delayed blow-back S.I.G. weapons of the 710-3 series firing the powerful N.A.T.O. 7.62 mm. round. The same guns could be installed on the bows of the launches that were carried by the black coaster.

The two small aircraft rushed to meet each other, the chopper passing above the climbing Cessna with a hundred feet to spare. There was no exchange of gunfire.

Ward watched the ground drop away beneath them as Fielding strained to gain precious altitude. The helicopter was turning again and on the second run Ward knew that there would be plenty of time for the pilot to line up his sights on the Cessna.

'They're coming in from behind,' he shouted to Fielding. 'Can't you get this bloody thing moving so we can outrun them?'

'Not until I can stop climbing then we'll leave them behind — keep your eye on them, I'm going to flatten out now.'

But the huge dragonfly was gaining.

'They're lining up to fire, Jack,' Ward

yelled. 'Turn, for God's sake turn!'

Above the roar of the Cessna's engine and the beating of the rotor on the pursuing helicopter, the staccato sound of the machine-guns filled Ward's ears. From the tubular under-carriage of the helicopter white flickering flames showed where the weapons were located. But there was no sound of tearing metal and no fire as there had been in the Widgeon. Firing from a range of over a thousand yards Shiga had been too hasty, the hail of lead missing the Cessna by less than six feet.

Before the helicopter could discharge more bullets, Fielding had stood the little monoplane on its right wing-tip in a fierce turn, pressing Ward hard against the side of the cockpit.

Still behind, the helicopter was continuing to close the gap.

Savagely Ward punched the muzzle of the Masden through the thick perspex of the rear window. 'Here they come again,' he said coldly. 'When I shout, start to change course.'

This time the helicopter had adopted a

different tactic. It rose fifty feet above the flight line of the Cessna and began to swoop downwards towards Ward.

At a range of six hundred feet, not knowing whether he stood any chance of hitting his target, Ward squeezed the trigger on the sub-machine gun aligning the barrel with the centre of the perspex bubble. Simultaneously, the S.I.G.s began to stutter out their message of death.

'Now,' Ward cried, 'now!'

Fielding had been watching the approach of the chopper over his shoulder and he knew that the difference in the speed of the two aircraft was now very much reduced. The Cessna was continuing to accelerate whilst the armed helicopter behind must already have reached its maximum velocity.

Steeling himself, he waited until the last second before sending his sixteen hundred pound aircraft into an impossible climb. At the same time Fielding yanked back on the throttle almost cutting the power from the engine.

His ammunition exhausted and with his body painfully compressed by the severe manoeuvre, Ward watched help-lessly as the bullets scythed half the tail plane away. He had experienced this before and he closed his eyes in anticipation of the sickening fiery dive that must follow.

But there had been cunning in Fielding's strategy. In a condition of total stall, the Cessna slipped backwards through the air like a poorly balanced paper aeroplane until the fuselage was nearly horizontal.

Unable to take avoiding action the helicopter passed underneath, its rotor flailing against the fixed undercarriage shrouds of the Cessna with explosive violence.

An awful scream of tortured metal echoed through the morning air high above Dublon island as the rotor disintegrated with an enormous bang, leaving the shattered remains of the main drive projecting at an oblique angle from behind the cockpit.

Its wings cruelly plucked off, the mortally wounded dragonfly stood upon its transparent and bulbous head before starting the terrible descent into the jungle below. Barely deviating from a completely vertical dive, the rotorless machine reached terminal velocity shortly before it smashed with unimaginable force into the unyielding earth. A ball of orange flame welled out from the point of impact, seeming to linger and flicker against the green background for several seconds before the smoke obliterated the scene.

Two thousand feet above, Fielding struggled desperately to regain control of the crippled Cessna. Using every technique that he had ever learnt, he fought against the sickening series of drifts that had been caused by his stall and by the deliberate collision with the helicopter. The aircraft was seven hundred feet lower by the time the pilot had managed to arrest the wandering motion and he was light-headed and exhausted from his exertions.

Thankful to be still alive, Ward allowed himself to breathe once more.

'I shall never ever fly again,' he announced at length. 'Especially with you — you're bloody mad!'

Fielding managed a weak grin. 'But I have delivered you twice from certain death,' he said. 'What about some gratitude, Mr. Ward.'

Ward was about to offer a suitable reply when he suddenly realised that they had made a dreadful mistake.

'Jack,' he yelled. 'The coaster, we're over the top of it!'

He had spoken too late.

Flashes of white flame erupted from the deck of the vessel below, the Oerlikons searching for the correct range.

Informed by radio from the helicopter only a few minutes ago, the skeleton crew that had remained on board the coaster had been forced to react hastily in manning their guns. It was the inexperience of the acting gunners that allowed the Cessna to narrowly escape the first burst of fire.

Not daring to subject the aircraft to any sudden manoeuvres with half the tail plane missing, Fielding did all that he could, executing a gentle turn to the left whilst gradually reducing the altitude that he had striven to gain such a little time ago.

'We'll never make it, Chris,' he shouted, 'I've got no control.'

With deadly precision the sights on the Oerlikons followed the helpless tiny aircraft, waiting for the moment when the pilot would have to stop his shallow dive.

Aware that the twenty millimetre shells would tear through the skin of the Cessna as though it was made of paper, both men clenched their teeth and waited for the end.

There was a sound like an axe sinking into a soft pine log and three feet of the starboard wing turned into a tangle of twisted metal, the shock kicking the aircraft sideways. Seconds later the engine exploded in a cloud of smoke. Oil sprayed from ruptured pipes to film the windshield.

'Ditch it, Jack,' Ward cried, remembering that the guns could not depress below a certain minimum angle.

But the heavy machine-guns had not yet finished their awful destruction. More of the tattered wing disappeared making it impossible for Fielding to maintain the dive.

Four hundred feet above the crystal clear water of Truk's lagoon, the pilot tried to stop the pathetic fluttering of what was left of his aircraft.

And then, through the oil smeared windshield, another larger vessel swam into view. As Ward and Fielding watched, two tongues of flame belched from the forward gun turret of the grey newcomer.

'It's a naval ship,' Ward yelled, almost unable to believe that help had miraculously arrived at last.

Fielding caught the most recent swoop of the Cessna, compensated for the inevitable slip in the opposite direction and pointed the shattered nose in the direction of the frigate he could see below.

The 115 mm. high explosive shells from the attacking Australian frigate ripped open the bowels of the coaster, a huge sheet of flame reaching fifty feet into the air. Replenished hydrogen cylinders used for filling the balloons had been brought on board some hours ago and, appropriately enough, it had been these that had blown the evil vessel asunder.

Buffeted by the shock wave, with no undercarriage, no engine and with her control surfaces shot away, the vestiges of the green and white Cessna 150 plunged downwards towards the unruffled texture of the waiting lagoon.

14

The afternoon sunshine was still too bright to allow the venetian blinds to be fully opened and the noise from Honolulu's traffic eight floors below made it equally unwise to open the window. Bored and frustrated, Christopher Ward shifted his position on the hospital bed so that he could see through the window between the slats.

There was a knock on the door and Fielding appeared, clothed as usual in a pair of flower patterned Hawaiian shorts and his bandages. He held a half empty bottle of whisky in his hand.

'Hi,' he said. 'You look as miserable as usual.'

Ward was glad to see him. 'At least you're allowed to walk about,' he said enviously, 'you'd be choked off too if you had to stay in bed.'

Fielding grinned at the Englishman. 'Only two more days, Chris, and then we're both going home.' He took a drink from his bottle.

Ward's recent experiences in the islands of the Pacific could easily have made him wish to return to England at once, however, having had plenty of time to think about it, he had decided that he was not yet ready to face London with the crowds, the traffic and the weather.

'You know what you said about me spending some time at Malolo Lailai?' he said slowly, 'did you mean it?'

The pilot's face lit up. 'Of course I did, Chris — nothing would please me more — there's a bure along the beach I can get for you — and a girl too.'

Ward grinned at his friend. 'Spare me the girl,' he said, 'this time I'm going to make sure my ribs join together properly.'

The military hospital in Honolulu had admitted Ward and Fielding nearly two weeks ago and this was the first day that the two men had not been subjected to questioning of some kind. It was perhaps this full day of relaxation that was causing Ward's boredom. After the extraordinary series of events he had experienced, he

285

was finding it surprisingly difficult to accept a very much more normal existence.

Fielding sat down on the bed just as another knock sounded on the door. He said 'Come in.'

Colonel Douglas entered the room.

Arriving in Honolulu one day after Ward and Fielding had been flown there from Truk in the Lockheed Jetstar of the American Airforce, Douglas had been responsible for leading the new phase of the enquiry, basking in his new found importance.

It had been Graham Redlands, the meteorological department head of P.D.3, who had persuaded Douglas to fight the authorities to further support their wild theories about M.P.173. The two men had again discussed the strange radio communication that had taken place with the innocent merchant vessel and, after stretching their imaginations, had concluded with remarkable accuracy that the *Doniambo* had been either deliberately or unknowingly used as a decoy.

For two days Redlands and Douglas

had worked to convince I.A.S. that another agent had been at work much closer to the point where M.P.173 had vanished. As the old met man had pointed out, the Colonel no longer had anything to lose and might just as well be hung for a sheep as a lamb. It was because Ralph Douglas had stared defeat and failure in the face that he was able to present his case so forcibly to Frank Macklin in Australia and to the Chiefs of Staff in Washington. Eventually, prepared to consider any suggestion that might lead to an explanation of the air disasters, the authorities had relented and agreed to organise an air search on a much more extensive scale.

Using an estimated time for the accident that Douglas had obtained from his tape recording, an unusual search pattern had been established. Flying in an expanding spiral, planes of the United States Airforce had used their radar to scan millions of square miles of ocean so that the course of all vessels in the reconnaissance zone could be plotted upon a master chart.

There had been only one ship — one solitary small ship that could have any suspicion whatever attached to her course. Her position on three successive days had been drawn on a map of the area and her speed calculated. By projecting her route backwards until it intersected with the flight path of the ill-fated D.C.8 of Malaysian Pacific, it had been an easy matter to show that the vessel had been in precisely the correct position at the right time.

The Australian frigate of P.D.1 that had intercepted the *Doniambo* had been instructed to make all speed in pursuit of the new suspect with orders to board the vessel as soon as she reached her final destination. If the frigate had not arrived at Truk when she did, Ward and Fielding would have died without knowing that the secret of Dublon island had been discovered at last. As it was, the boat that had been dispatched from the frigate to pick up the two men from the Cessna had reached them only seconds before the ruined aircraft had sunk.

The subsequent round up of the

members of Shiga's organisation had been no simple matter in the dense jungle, but Dublon was surrounded by water and more than two hundred men had been employed in the final phase of the operation — after three days it had all been over. Colonel Ralph Douglas had never been so elated in his life before.

Now he greeted the two men that he had come to know so well, noting that Ward seemed rather more dull than usual.

'What's the trouble, Chris?' he asked.

'Just tired of hospital,' Ward replied. 'I had enough of it in L.A.'

The Colonel waved a finger at him. 'Hell,' he said. 'It's only for another couple of days, then we'll let you go home to London. You can recuperate properly there.'

'I am not going home to England, I'm going back with Jack to Fiji.'

Douglas appeared to disapprove. 'I'm not sure that's such a good idea,' he said.

Ward grinned at him. 'Stop being so bloody pompous,' he said. 'The whole thing's gone to your head and you've forgotten I'm a civilian — I'll do what I want to.'

'What about I.A.S.?'

Ward shrugged. 'I'm not even sure I want to go back there — I want a holiday first anyway — then I'll decide.'

Fielding interrupted the conversation. 'Do you think I might lead him astray, Colonel?' he said, an artificially serious expression on his face.

Douglas looked sternly at the pilot. 'I'm quite sure you will,' he said, 'that's probably what he wants.'

The pilot smiled at the older man. 'I'll look after him,' he said.

'I do not want looking after,' Ward shouted angrily.

Douglas consulted his watch. 'Come on downstairs, Jack,' he said. 'I want to talk to you about the government compensation for your Widgeon — and throw away that whisky, you drunken bum!'

'I don't want cash,' Fielding said. 'I've already told you that — I want another plane.' He took another long drink, draining the bottle.

A pained expression crossed the Colonel's face. 'If you come downstairs — now — perhaps you might even get both.' He walked to the door waiting for Fielding to follow him.

The pilot casually waved a hand to Ward. 'See you for dinner, Chris.'

Left alone again, Ward turned awkwardly onto his stomach, switched on the bedside radio and closed his eyes.

Several minutes passed before he became aware of a faint smell of perfume. He opened one eye.

Staring anxiously down at him, her face pale but still beautiful, Joanne was relieved to find that he was not asleep.

Struggling to sit up, Ward could not believe that she was here.

'Jo,' he stuttered, 'oh, Jo.'

She bent down to kiss him.

It was some time before either of them noticed the heads of Douglas and the pilot peering amusedly round the door.

'You bastards,' Ward yelled at them. 'Why didn't you tell me?'

'I've booked two seats to Fiji in your

name,' Fielding said grinning. 'Is that okay?'

Ward nodded at him. 'That is very okay,' he said. 'Now get the hell out of here — both of you — I'm busy.'

THE END

THAT INFERNAL TRIANGLE

Mark Ashton

An aeroplane goes down in the notorious Bermuda Triangle and on board is an Englishman recently heavily insured. The suspicious insurance company calls in Dan Felsen, former RAF pilot turned private investigator. Dan soon runs into trouble, which makes him suspect the infernal triangle is being used as a front for a much more sinister reason for the disappearance. His search for clues leads him to the Bahamas, the Caribbean and into a hurricane before he resolves the mystery.

THE GUILTY WITNESSES

John Newton Chance

Jonathan Blake had become involved in finding out just who had stolen a precious statuette. A gang of amateurs had so clever a plot that they had attracted the attention of a group of international spies, who habitually used amateurs as guide dogs to secret places of treasure and other things. Then, of course, the amateurs were disposed of. Jonathan Blake found himself being shot at because the guide dogs had lost their way . . .

THIS SIDE OF HELL

Robert Charles

Corporal David Canning buried his best friend below the burning African sand. Then he was alone, with a bullet-sprayed ambulance containing five seriously injured men and one hysterical nurse in his care. He faced heat, dust, thirst and hunger; and somewhere in the area roamed almost two hundred blood-crazed tribesmen led by a white mercenary with his own desperate reasons for catching up with the sole survivors of the massacre. But Canning vowed that he would win through to safety.